Edgar Wallace was born illegitima
adopted by George Freeman, a port
eleven, Wallace sold newspapers at
school took a job with a printer. He enlisted in the Royal West Kent
Regiment, later transferring to the Medical Staff Corps, and was sent
to South Africa. In 1898 he published a collection of poems called
The Mission that Failed, left the army and became a correspondent
for Reuters.

Wallace became the South African war correspondent for *The
Daily Mail*. His articles were later published as *Unofficial Dispatches* and
his outspokenness infuriated Kitchener, who banned him as a war
correspondent until the First World War. He edited the *Rand Daily
Mail*, but gambled disastrously on the South African Stock Market,
returning to England to report on crimes and hanging trials. He
became editor of *The Evening News*, then in 1905 founded the Tallis
Press, publishing *Smithy*, a collection of soldier stories, and *Four Just
Men*. At various times he worked on *The Standard*, *The Star*, *The Week-
End Racing Supplement* and *The Story Journal*.

In 1917 he became a Special Constable at Lincoln's Inn and also
a special interrogator for the War Office. His first marriage to Ivy
Caldecott, daughter of a missionary, had ended in divorce and he
married his much younger secretary, Violet King.

The Daily Mail sent Wallace to investigate atrocities in the Belgian
Congo, a trip that provided material for his *Sanders of the River* books.
In 1923 he became Chairman of the Press Club and in 1931 stood as
a Liberal candidate at Blackpool. On being offered a scriptwriting
contract at RKO, Wallace went to Hollywood. He died in 1932, on
his way to work on the screenplay for *King Kong*.

Good Evans

HOUSE OF
STRATUS

This edition published in 2001 by House of Stratus, an imprint of
House of Stratus Ltd, Thirsk Industrial Park, York Road, Thirsk,
North Yorkshire, YO7 3BX, UK.

www.houseofstratus.com

Typeset by House of Stratus, printed and bound by Short Run Press Limited.

A catalogue record for this book is available from the British Library
and the Library of Congress.

ISBN 1-84232-687-2

We would like to thank the Edgar Wallace Society for all the support they have given
House of Stratus. Enquiries on how to join the Edgar Wallace Society should be addressed to:
The Edgar Wallace Society, c/o Penny Wyrd, 84 Ridgefield Road, Oxford, OX4 3DA.
Email: info@edgarwallace.org Web: http://www.edgarwallace.org/

CONTENTS

A CHANGE OF PLAN

It was when an excited and vengeful client demanded what the so-and-so and such a thing Mr Evans meant by sending out three selections for one race, that the educated man laid down his system of ethics.

"Tippin'," he said, "is tactics. You start out to do one thing an' do another. Bettin's a battle. You got to change your plans the same as the celebrated Napoleon Bonaparte, him that was killed in the Battle of Waterloo."

This philosophy he impressed upon a Miss Casey, with disastrous effects. As to Miss Casey…

To sit beside a beautiful lady at the cinema is indeed a privilege. To feel her small hand steal into yours in the excitement and emotion occasioned by the film, is thrilling. Educated Evans had both these experiences. The lady was young and beautiful and she had large grey eyes…presently to be blinded with hot tears at the pitiable plight of Madame X.

Evans returned the grip of her hand and reeled. "Whatever will you think of me?" she asked penitently as they came out of the cinema.

"My opinion of you," said Mr Evans passionately, "is the same as the well-known Henry the Eighth had for the far-famed Joan of Arc."

"Oh, go on!" said the delighted Miss Casey.

They went to a famous corner shop café and Evans blew ten bob on coffee and doughnuts and a box of chocolates tied up with blue ribbon – which was Miss Casey's favourite colour.

Mr Evans agreed to meet her in Hyde Park the following evening, and went home walking on air.

A week later Mr Challoner – The Miller to the cognoscenti of Camden Town – called on the educated man. And the real reason for his call was an article in a certain weekly publication. The article was entitled 'Fortunes from Tipping,' and the paragraph ran:

Another turf prophet who has amassed wealth is Mr Evans, the well-known racing man of Camden Town. Although Mr Evans lives in unostentatious surroundings, it is no secret that his fortune runs into five figures.

"Did you supply that information?" asked The Miller sternly.

"It's publicity or press work," murmured Evans. "I had a chat with the reporter – met him up West – "

"Five figures!" said The Miller, shocked.

"Ten pun' nine an' eleven," said Evans calmly. "Write that down an' if it ain't five figures nothin' is."

He had been putting the finishing touch to a neat little sign on the door – an oblong of wood on which was painted the new house title.

No directory of Camden Town would reveal the whereabouts of 'Priory Park' but for the fact that on all circulars to clients, old and new, Mr Evans added more concisely, 'Bayham Mews, NW.'

"You've got a nerve," said The Miller with that reluctant admiration he offered to the successful criminal. "So far as I can remember, your tip was Asterus."

Educated Evans closed his eyes, a sure sign of offended dignity, and began to search the one drawer of an article which served as desk, counter, dressing-table, stand for duplicator and, occasionally, seat. From the litter the drawer contained he produced a duplicated sheet.

"Read," he said simply.

Detective Inspector Challoner read.

EDUCATED EVANS!
The World's Chief Turf Adviser
(Under Royal Patronage)
To all clients I advise a good bet on
ASTERUS★★★

At the same time I am warned by my correspondents that Weissdorn is greatly fancied and that King of Clubs will be on the premises. At the same time what beats Melon will win and Priory Park will run forward.

"He ran forward," said Mr Evans with even greater simplicity.

"Most horses do," said The Miller, "unless they're clothes horses."

"I also give Sprig – what a double!"

"Sprig? You lie in your boots!" said the indignant Miller.

Evans shook his head.

"Sprig," he said. "I've got documents to prove that me Ten Pun' Special to all and sundried was Sprig – fear nothing."

The Miller did not argue. Mr Evans' Ten Pound Special was his favourite myth; there was no such thing.

Once upon a time Evans had announced his intention of sending out such a startling service, and had offered it for a beggarly quid a nod, but nobody coughed up and the service fell into disuse. For why, argued the regulars who followed Educated Evans to their ruin, pay a pound for a ten pun' special when you could get his five pound guarantee wire for a dollar – and that on the nod?

"Them Lubeses is givin' me trouble, Mr Challoner," said Evans, shaking his head sadly. "I've done me best to educate the woman but she's like the far-famed horse that could be led to the slaughter but you couldn't make him think. Never since the days of Mary Queen of Scotch – her that invented the well-known Johnny Walker – has there been a lady like Mrs Lube – an' when I call her a lady I expect to be struck down for perjury."

The Miller lingered on the first step of the ladder by which Mr Evans reached Priory Park.

"It's malice an' libel this time – an' mind you, Mr Challoner, I haven't said a word about her new lodger – but she's takin' the name of a young lady in vain – as good a young lady as ever drew the breath of life!"

The Miller came back to the room.

"You interest me strangely," he said. "Who is the unfortunate female honoured by your attentions at the moment?"

The face of Mr Evans went pink; his manner became haughty, almost cold.

"She's in business down the West End an' it's purely planetic."

"What-ic?" asked the puzzled inspector, and then: "Oh – you mean platonic."

"It's spelt both ways," said Evans, unmoved. "The Germans call it one thing and the French another. The whole proceedings are accordin' to what you've been brought up to. I call it planetic."

The Miller did not pursue this shameless change of pronunciation but pursued his enquiries.

"I am anxious to know," he said, "because my experience is that women only get hold of you to twist you – what's she after?"

Evans smiled.

"We got an infinity for one another," he said. "She's in lingery."

"Let us be delicate," said Mr Challoner.

"I mean she's in a lingery department of Snodds and Richersens, the well-known high class shop – see advertisements. I met her the day I brought off All Green – fear nothin' – what a beauty! In fact we was seein' a film at the Hippodrome and I lent her a handkerchief to wipe away her tears. She's Irish on her father's side, but her mother's quite a lady. Them Lubeses see me with her at the cinema and put it around I was adoptin' her. An' I've had anomolous letters callin' me a body snatcher."

"From which I gather that she is young," said The Miller.

"Twenty come the nineteenth of April," said Mr Evans. "And what an education! She knows Romeo and Julia, Switzerland, where all the well-known winter sports go to, hist'ry an' grammar an' she can knit ties."

"Has she got medals for these accomplishments?" asked the sarcastic police officer.

"Cups," said Evans, and added: "She can play the pianner with two fingers."

Mr Evans could afford a little light recreation. Since the five-figure episode he had struck a vein of fortune such as come to few tipsters. He had not only tipped three winners off the reel, but he had, with unexampled recklessness or courage, backed them. As Mr Issyheim said when he reluctantly counted out note after note into the trembling hands of the world's supreme prophet and turf adviser, all the miracles were going against the book.

Evans had a new suit – or practically so. It was, in hue, violently blue, the trousers were slightly long in the leg, even when painfully braced, but the general effect was distinctly classy. A new hat and tie usually sacred to the officers of the 10th Hussars completed the pleasing picture when, on a bright spring morning, Evans journeyed by bus to Paddington Station.

A neat little figure awaited him in the booking-hall. Awaited? Nay, came running towards him.

"I've bought the tickets!" she said excitedly. "Oh, Mr Evans, I've got so much to tell you!"

He winced at the sight of the tickets – they were first-class; but her next words reassured him.

"I insist on paying for the tickets. Mr Evans – I'm rich!"

He smiled tolerantly. Nothing made Mr Evans smile so tolerantly as somebody else paying.

"They wouldn't give me special tickets," she said. "I told them you were a member of the Jockey Club – "

"In a sense," said Evans hastily, as he hurried her to the platform. "It's not generally known. I do a lot of secret service work for the old club – that's why I usually go into the silver ring. Me an' Lonsdale's like brothers – good mornin', me lord!"

He lifted his hat graciously to a hurrying race-goer. The hurrying race-goer nodded and said "Hullo, face!" and passed on.

They had a carriage to themselves. The Miller, walking along the platform, paused at the door but thought better of it.

"Now!" said Eileen Casey as the train started. "What do you think of this?"

She produced from her bag a long envelope. It had been heavily sealed in wax. Pulling out a letter, she handed it triumphantly to Evans. The letterhead ran:

> John Dougherty, Solicitors, Ballyriggan,
> Co. Wexford.

DEAR MISS CASEY,

We have had a communication from Heinz and Heinz, Attorneys, 175 Fifth Avenue, New York, of which we hasten to apprise you. By the will of your uncle John Donovan Casey (deceased) the sum of $100,000 and the residue of his estate (proved at $1,757,000) is bequeathed to you...

Evans gasped and the lines swam before his eyes. In his agitation he held her hand.

...absolutely. The attorneys inform me that it will be necessary that you should go to New York at once. As I know you are in possession of the necessary funds, it is not necessary to offer you an advance on account of expenses. Our Mr Michael Dougherty will join you at Queenstown.

"Well, well, well!" said Evans.

But apparently it was not well.

"You see, Mr Evans, I've been rather a fool – I didn't want my people at Ballyriggan to know that I was a shop girl, and so I – well, I showed off. You'll never understand that."

Mr Evans understood perfectly.

"You got your position to keep up," he said, "the same as me. Everybody's swankers. Take Pharer's daughter, her that said she found the well-known Moses in the bullrushes, take Queen Elizabeth, the far-famed verging queen, take B— Mary, her that done in her little nephews in the Tower…"

He talked all the time and his busy brain was working overtime. He saw the fulfilment of his ambitions. He would buy Swan and Edgar's and put up a twenty storey building with Educated Evans picked out in black marble. He'd have a grand dining room and invite the trainers who, under the influence of generous wines, would put him on to the goods. His advertisements would cover front pages.

EVENTUALLY – WHY NOT NOW?
EDUCATED EVANS
Piccadilly Circus
(same address for thirty years)
Verb Sap.
(Enough Said).

In this exalted mood came Mr Evans to Newbury. "Don't waste your money," said the young lady anxiously.

But nothing would hold Mr Evans.

"I got a horse in the first race that can't lose unless the stewards are cuttin' it up. I got him from the boy that does him. He's been tried better than Pri'ry Park – an' there's one in the three o'clock that could fall down, and get up an' then win. I got him from me man at Lambourn. I got agents everywhere."

"Don't lose your money," warned Miss Casey…

£80 to £20 the first winner, 100-15 the third, 200-25 the fourth.

Returning by train, there was little opportunity for confidences. At the little restaurant near King's Cross Evans bought a bottle of wine and they talked. From this man of the world she had much advice.

"Don't be puttin' your money in banks," he said. "Hand it over to some educated person of experience. Look how banks fail…"

He explained his own methods of securing his wealth; showed her the pocket inside his waistcoat.

"Now about this fortune of yours, Miss Casey. I can let you have the money to get to America – "

"I wouldn't dream of it!" she said instantly, and the little nagging worry that had gnawed at Evans' heart all day vanished. "I've got enough and more than enough – but you are a darling."

Evans closed his eyes and breathed through his nose. Nobody had called him a darling for years, though Mrs Lube had once addressed him as 'a pretty beauty.' Probably she did not mean it.

"I should so love to see your office," she said suddenly.

Mr Evans coughed.

"It's not much to look at," he admitted, "but if you go puttin' up skyscrapers you only attract a lot of undesirables, as the saying goes. They just call in for a drink an' that's where your profit goes."

Nevertheless, he allowed himself to be persuaded.

"What a dear little room!" She was bright-eyed and ecstatic. "I suppose you keep your race-horses in the stables downstairs?"

In the 'stables' downstairs was a Ford van, the property of a provision merchant, but Mr Evans did not think it necessary to explain this.

They sat together, he smoking one of her scented cigarettes, and they discussed the future.

"I'm rather young to marry," she said, "but I should feel safe with you, Algernon. And having all this money…"

"Qui' ri'," said Mr Evans thickly.

Two days later The Miller, strolling up West and entirely out of his own division, was called upon to assist two policemen in the arrest of a certain Mr Albert Ugger, on a charge of working the confidence trick on an unsuspecting American. Mr Ugger was ferociously intoxicated, but under the beneficent influence of The Miller, whom he recognized, he went quietly.

"Wimmin's ruined me, Miller," he said as they marched him to Vine Street. "I got a mug taped up Camden Town way – a feller called Evans. He's got lashins of money accordin' to the papers…"

The Miller was a fascinated audience.

"… So we put Polly Agathy on to him – she's twenty-eight but looks a kid…and what do you think she done on us? Gave him a doped fag and skipped out with four hundred quid that she took from his pouch. Is that right – I ask yer?"

The Miller began to understand why for the past two days no selections had been flowing from the anguished tenant of Priory Park.

MR EVANS DOES A BIT OF GAS-WORK

Mr Siniter was wider than Broad Street. He was very rich and he trusted nobody, least of all jockeys. But he thought he could trust Lem Dooby, one of the smartest lads that ever left Australia for the good of the English turf. That a jockey could not trust Siniter will be made clear.

Lem had rather a pretty wife. Saul Siniter had a soft place in his heart for beauty, married or unmarried; and Lem's wife had a weakness for good dinners, parties, and those expensive but inconspicuous articles of jewellery that a very rich bookmaker could, with propriety, send her on her birthday.

One day, when Lem was riding in the North, Mrs Lem and Saul dined magnificently, danced till three o'clock in the morning, at which hour Saul saw her home.

"I'll tell you the truth, Saul," said Margarita, which was her name: "I'm rather worried about Lem. He's one of those quiet people who say nothing and think a lot; and if he should hear – "

"Don't worry about Lem," scoffed Mr Siniter, who was a very tall, handsome man with the manner of a duke – such dukes as have manners. "Unless you go talking, Lem will know nothing. Anyway, I'll write to him tomorrow, and tell him I took you out to dinner, so there's no secret about it."

Which was very true. There was no secret at all about the dinner part of the evening or even the dancing part.

Mr Siniter, for all his bulk and his strength and his notorious *savoir faire*, was a moral coward, of the type to whom worry and suspicion were more potent poisons than strychnine and arsenic. For the moment, however, he saw no cause to worry: he had a horse that was saved for one of the big handicaps, and which he had backed at ridiculous odds; he had a certain winner in Hot Feet when the moment arrived to let his head loose; and he could contemplate the future with equanimity.

Before Hot Feet ran at Hurst he had a little conversation with Lem Dooby, who was a very nice little man without vice or temperament.

"Lem," he said, "I don't want you to win this race...yes, I know they'll make him favourite, but seven to four is no good to me. I've told everybody to back him and the next time we'll get a good price. You'd better get caught flat-footed at the start, and the further you're left the better I shall be pleased."

Lem nodded.

But he was a man who had many friends, in all circles of society; and as he was going into the ring he saw a nobleman for whom he had ridden and who he knew was in that select circle which supplies the stewards of meetings all over the country.

"I want to talk to you, Dooby," he said, and led the jockey aside. "You must tell nobody, not your best friend, what I'm telling you, but there's been a lot of talk about the way Siniter rubs out, and they're watching your running today very carefully. In fact, one of the stewards will be down at the elbow to see the start. You can make any excuse you like to Siniter – and I know I can trust you not to tell him the truth – but I don't want to see you stood down."

Lem, who was a wise lad, touched his cap and went into the saddling-ring.

The story of Hot Feet's possibilities was already public property in Camden Town.

The Miller met Evans at the corner of Bayham Street.

"One of these days," he said savagely, "you're going to get me hung; and if you don't get me, you'll get yourself hung. What the devil do you mean by calling up the police station and telling the sergeant that you had something hot and extra for me?"

Evans shrugged his shoulders.

"You've been a good friend of mine, Mr Challoner," he said, "and I wasn't going to let you drop out of this coop. I got it this morning from a feller that does a lot of betting at the club, an' I promised him I wouldn't tell a soul."

"And you sent it out to your forty-three thousand clients, I presume?" said The Miller.

"Five hundred an' seventy-four," confessed Evans, in a modest vein. "I've been sendin' an army of messengers all over Camden Town puttin' them on to Hot Feet."

"A bookmaker's horse," said The Miller coldly. "It's the sort of stumer that bookmakers put around. Hot Feet! Cold Feet would be a better name for him!"

Mr Evans smiled cryptically.

"He's been tried forty-one pounds – " he began.

The Miller silenced him with a look.

Apparently the legend that Hot Feet was a stumer, and that Evans was the misguided, perhaps the all too willing, victim of a pencillers' machinations, was for some extraordinary reason general throughout Camden Town. When Mr Evans took the air at midday in the High Street he was accosted every few yards by sceptical clients.

"What's this Hot Feet you've sent me. Evans? Siniter's horse! I'm surprised at you sending a wire like that. He was beat a short head at Hurst and he'll be rubbin' out today."

Evans closed his eyes and looked pained. A few yards on he met Mr Harriboy, the far-famed fishmonger and poulterer.

"I've get your message, Mr Evans, but I can't see Hot Feet winning. He's a bookmaker's horse, and everybody knows he'll be rubbin' out today."

Now rubbing out, as the initiated know, is the art of discouraging backers from putting their money on horses that seem to have an outstanding chance. And this art is very widely practised. Today you are a short head behind a good winner; next week your horse starts at 6-4 and finishes a bad fourth; and this may happen on his next outing, until newspaper tipsters and wily punters grow weary of supporting this erratic animal; and then he pops up at a price remunerative to all concerned. And Mr Siniter was one of the best known rubbers out of form.

"I can only tell you," said Evans patiently, "that he's On the Job. If there's any man in Camden Town who can teach me my business, let him come forward or for ever hold his speech. I'll allow him ten points for education an' then beat him. I'm like the far-famed salamander, I've got eyes in the back of me head – I've got to, Mr Harriboy, to live."

Mr Harriboy shook his head.

"I'm not backing your horse today, Evans," he said definitely.

And others had formed a conclusion as definite; and when, that afternoon, Hot Feet won at 7-1, there were sore hearts in Camden Town.

"It's Evans' fault," said Mr Harriboy to a disgruntled friend. "If he'd only told us what he knew, instead of chucking his weight about up and down High Street, I'd have been on that horse."

After the race Lem got down to meet his enraged owner.

"What the hell do you mean by winning?" hissed Siniter. "Didn't I tell you that I'd not backed the horse? Didn't I ask you to start flat-footed?"

"I was left, but I couldn't hold him in," said Lem, and for two pins would have told him the strength of the position, but loyalty to his aristocratic friend kept him silent.

Mr Siniter went away from the course a very thoughtful man; and two days later, when he met Margarita, expressed his suspicion.

"Lem's got something at the back of his mind. I don't think you and I had better be seen out together so much. I'll have to find another jockey."

Now Margarita was not a nice woman, but she had a curious sense of loyalty.

"You'll do nothing of the kind," she said. "Lem never did a crooked thing in his life."

Mr Siniter grew purple.

"He's not going to ride Blue Tick!" he stormed. "I've backed him to win me three thousand and I'm taking no risks."

She smiled.

"You don't know what risks you'll be taking if you put down Lem," she said significantly.

He very wisely did not ask questions. And later that day it came to his ears that one Educated Evans had sent Hot Feet to 49,732 clients, of which five had backed the horse and fifteen hadn't.

Mr Siniter trusted no detective. He himself went in search of Educated Evans and found him engaged in the preparation of his morning advice.

"Sorry to intrude on you, mister," said the temporarily genial Siniter.

He looked round the apartment. It did not seem the kind of place from which 49,732 letters were likely to be addressed, but you never know what tipsters can do at a push.

"I've come to thank you for your tip on Hot Feet," said Mr Siniter, and put a five-pound note on the table. "You sent it to a friend of mine, but I backed it. Now if you ever have any tips from this stable – "

"I have 'em every day," said Mr Evans with a quiet smile. "There's nothin' that twistin' Siniter does that I don't know."

Siniter swallowed.

"You knew that Hot Feet was going to win?" he said, maintaining his calm with difficulty.

Evans nodded. "Information *v*. gasworks," he said. "I got a boy in the stable, and Dooby – "

"Ah – you know Dooby, I suppose?"

Evans smiled again.

"Me an' him's like brothers," he said. "I met him at the Jockey Club in Park Lane. He reminds me of the celebrated Fred Archer who rode the far-famed Eclipse when it won at Sandown Park in 1795 – I don't know whether it was the fourth or fifth of May."

"You know a lot about Mr Siniter's horses?"

Educated Evans was amused.

"Everything," he said. "Take Blue Tick – him they lay 7-4 about in the Escom Handicap – not a yard!"

Mr Siniter heard and perspired.

"What – who told you?" he demanded, trying to smother his wrath.

"Information," murmured Evans. "That race is a squinch for Dewflower – tried two stone better than Lopear an' walked it!"

When Mr Siniter got home he summoned Lem by phone.

"Dooby, I'm putting up another jockey on Blue Tick. I don't think you understand the horse, old man."

Dooby understood.

"Certainly," he said. "Now who shall we put up? What about Jim Gold?"

Now the name of Jim Gold had also occurred to Mr Siniter, but the mere fact that Dooby suggested it was quite sufficient to put him off.

"No, I can't have Jim: he wouldn't ride one side of the horse," he said. "I don't mind any other jockey – bar Slick Markey."

Here again Lem understood. Slick Markey was as crooked as a flash of lightning. Even jockeys, who never give one another away, admitted that Slick was mustard. He was one of these clever jockeys who got twenty-five mounts a year and was popularly supposed to be in everybody's pocket but his own.

"No, I wouldn't advise you to take Slick – he can't help thieving any more than I can help scratching my head. What about Tommy Lutter?"

Mr Siniter hesitated. It had been on the tip of his tongue to mention the same jockey.

"No," he said, "he doesn't understand the horse either. I don't care who rides him, but the only thing I bar is Slick."

"Naturally," murmured the sympathetic Dooby.

He went away without having discovered a solution to the pressing problem. By midnight Siniter had worked himself into a condition of nervous prostration, and at that hour he called up someone who was nearly a friend.

"I want a jockey to ride my horse Blue Tick," he said. "I don't think he'll win, but he's a curious horse to ride and I'd like to have the best man available."

His friend, who was also an owner, thought for some time.

"Isn't Dooby riding – no? Well, what about Joe Ginnett? He hasn't a mount. Funnily enough, I saw him tonight in Camden Town – "

"Oh, did you?" said Siniter loudly. "Well, he won't do! Can you suggest anybody else?"

After a long pause, "I don't know…of course you can't have Slick: he's impossible. If he knew you'd backed the horse he'd stop it, and if you hadn't backed it he'd win. And he's in the pocket of…" He libelled half a dozen perfectly respectable but eminent pencillers of Tattersalls. "The only man I can suggest is Callison. He's a friend of Dooby's – "

"He won't do either," said Mr Siniter promptly. "Sorry to bother you, old man – I'll think it out."

"Anyway, don't take Slick," came the final warning. Mr Siniter, in spite of his agitation, smiled.

Time was growing short. The next day he made another attempt. One jockey after another came up for review – none could be trusted. At eleven o'clock that night he rang up Slick Markey and offered him the mount.

Secretly, and in an assumed name, he had become one of Mr Evans' subscribers. The morning post brought a communication from that genius.

EDUCATED EVANS,
The World's Premier Prophet & Turf Adviser.
KEEP OFF BLUE TICK!
KEEP OFF BLUE TICK!
KEEP OFF BLUE TICK!
Information *v.* Gaswork

> Straight from a reliable source. My information is that
> BEGGAR BOY★★★
> is walking over for the important event as advertised
> in all leading papers.

Mr Siniter wiped his perspiring brow. Somebody knew more than he; there was a conspiracy amongst these jockeys. What a fool he had been to put up Slick, the most notorious crook of all!

To change him now was neither possible nor desirable. There was only one thing to do. He sent secret instructions to his commission agents to lay Blue Tick, and drove to the course with the full assurance that he had taken the right action.

Before the race he interviewed the wizen-faced jockey with the shifty eyes.

"I've laid off all my bets on this horse," he said, "so you can handle him gently."

Slick nodded – he was a man of very few words, and they were mostly unprintable.

There was a big field. Mr Evans, lounging against the rails, waited with a calm air of assurance for his unbeatable gem to materialize.

He never could read a race, and never learnt to look at any of the horses except the one he had backed – and usually he confounded that with another.

There was no mistaking Blue Tick: he was a grey, and the flamboyant colours of Mr Siniter could not be mistaken nor confounded with anything more delicate. They lay in the centre of the field, about third for most of the journey. In the last furlong they drew to the front…

Blue Tick won, hard held, by three lengths.

"Information *v.* gaswork," said Evans bitterly. "It almost makes you give up trying to find 'em!"

Mr Siniter watched the horses come back to the paddock like a man in a dream. And it was a pretty bad dream. He saw Dooby, who rode one of the last division, slip from his horse and unsaddle, and as the little man passed him Mr Siniter noticed in a vague kind of way that he was beaming.

"I'm glad you won, guv'nor," said the jockey. "I think anybody could have won on him. He had us beat from start to finish. I hope you had a good win. My missis had eighty pounds on him."

Mr Siniter recovered his voice.

"Who told her to back it?" he asked hollowly.

"Old Slick Markey, just before he went out," said Lem. "It's given me another idea of old Slick – first time I've ever known him to do the straight thing."

EDUCATION AND COMBINATIONS

Mr Evans had concluded his ablutions and had hung the towel on the bed-rail to dry. The yellow sunlight which slanted through the open window proclaimed the coming of spring; the piles of unopened letters that covered the table proclaimed the Turn of the Tide.

Until the small hours of the morning he had been turning the handle of the Duplicating Machine that a Child Could Work, and littering the bed was his latest *pronunciamento*.

EDUCATED EVANS!
The World's Premier Profit and Turf Adviser.
(Thirty-five years at the same address)
STICKY BOY (7-1) What a beauty!!
STICKY BOY (7-1) What a beauty!!
STICKY BOY (7-1) What a beauty!!

Once more the well-beloved Evans has done the hat trick by giving a 7-1 winner – nothing else mentioned!!

Information *v.* Gaswork!

Now I want all clients new and old to roll up in their millions for the grandest winner that ever looked through a bridal! This one will win the

NEWBURY CUP.
He's been tried unbeatable!
He's been tried unbeatable!

Eventually – why not now?
Eventually – why not now?
Send PO 5s for this Guaranteed £5 Special. Special to Educated
Evans, Myra Gray Mansions, Bayham Mews, NW.

Evans picked up a duplicated sheet and read it with satisfaction. He had struck a blow at the very heart of his enemies. Seven successive three star naps had Old Sam sent forth in his Midnight Special, and each and every one of them had gone down the sink.

He heard footsteps on the stairs, but he did not turn round, even when a shadow came into the room.

"Good morning, Mr Evans."

The educated man spun round and his face went pale. Standing in the doorway was Mrs Lube, and in her hand a large bunch of primroses.

"Many happy returns of the day, Mr Evans, an' let by-gorns be by-gorns."

Once you knew Mr Evans' birthday it was well nigh impossible to forget it, for he first saw light on April 1st in the year – well, never mind about the year.

"Um – same to you, Mrs Lube."

He took the flowers gingerly, expecting them to explode at any moment.

"May I come in, Mr Evans?"

He indicated a chair and watched her warily, ready to jump at the first sign of a poker. But not only was Mrs Lube unarmed, she was disarming.

"I daresay you wonder why I come, Mr Evans," she said. "After all the bickerin' an' unpleasantness we've had and what not. But what I say is live an' let live but I've been talking it over with my dear gran'father an' my dear husband an' I says 'What's the use of us tryin' to down dear Mr Evans?' I says, 'the only thing to do,' I says, 'is to get him to help us,' I says."

Evans found his voice gruffly.

"I got nothing to give away," he said.

Mrs Lube swallowed.

"Yes, you have, Mr Evans." She was very earnest, or appeared to be. "You've got education. I says to my poor dear gran'father, 'What's the use of our goin' on as we're goin' on without education?' "

Educated Evans coughed and fingered his chin importantly.

"I says," continued Mrs Lube, "the only thing is to throw ourselves on his mercy an' for me to ask him to educate me."

Evans coughed again.

"In a manner of speakin' you're right," he said. "Take biology an' science. What's water? In French it's 'O.' In science it's H_3O, in German it's something altogether different. Take the world, which revolves or turns on its axle once in every twenty-four hours, thus causin' the stars to shine. Take history. The War of the Roses was caused through Lancashire beatin' Yorkshire and vicer verser, which is Latin. Which brings us to Julia Caesar, the far-famed wife that was always suspicious of her husband owin' to his carryin' on with Lewdcreature Burgia, the female Crippen of Italy. Where's Italy, you ask me? That's geography again and brings us to the question of Mussell Enos, the far-famed Fassykist that was."

Mrs Lube blinked rapidly.

"My poor brain!" she said disparagingly. "What a headpiece you've got, Mr Evans!"

"Take botomy, the science of vegetables," said Evans, warming to his subject. "By studyin' the ways an' means of flowers we arrive at zoo-ology or caterpillars which change into butterflies by metamorphious methods commonly called hibernation..."

Mrs Lube stayed two hours and had a grounding in erudition.

"It's your idea, Alfred," she said to her husband on her return, "and if it turns out that I've bin wastin' my time on that old so-and-so, I'll have something to say to you!"

"We've got to do something," said Alfred.

Detective-Inspector Arbuthnot Challoner was taking what was literally and figuratively a constitutional. In other words he was engaged in the improvement of his system by the exercise of his limbs and the improvement of Camden Town by the employment of his senses.

He called at the Blue Pig, to the embarrassment of a young married gentleman who was greatly in arrears with his wife's maintenance; he looked in at Hookey's Coffee Bar and Good Pull Up for Carman and found Spicey Brown and Cully Parks intent on dominoes – they invariably planned their busts over a game, and used the pieces to model the house they intended to burgle.

("Say that double-six is the front door," Cully was saying when The Miller arrived, "and that four-one is the pantry winder, all we gotter do is to get down the area an' the job's as good as done...")

The pieces were swept into confusion on The Miller's approach, and two innocent men greeted him with sycophantic pleasure.

Mr Challoner's next call was at a fried-fish shop off the High Street, where one who was born Lieverbaum but was now styled Leverbrown carried on a small spieling club in the back parlour.

Comparatively speaking, Camden Town was law-abiding and almost chaste.

"All the boys have gorn racin', Mr Challoner," said Lieverbaum, rubbing his podgy hands. "It's a blessing this racing, ain't it? Keeps the boys out of mischief – yes? An' what with Edjercated Evings doin' so well – three winners right orf the reel – the man's marvellous! The bookmakers are doin' rotten."

He spoke feelingly, for Mr Lieverbaum was notoriously an evader of the law, being an unlicensed bookmaker, and had been three times convicted.

The Miller stopped long enough to warn him against this practice, and resumed his stroll. And then, turning past the Nag's Head in the direction of Regents Park, he beheld a sight which left him dazed and gasping. There flashed past him one of these expensive cars which can be hired by the mile or by the hour, and wedged on the back seat thereof was Mrs Lube, a white-bearded old gentleman, and Mr Evans of Myra Gray Mansions.

The Miller's first thought was that his unfortunate friend had been kidnapped, and his hand strayed to his pocket where he kept his whistle. In another second the car had vanished in the direction of the park.

That evening, being off duty, he made a call in Bayham Mews and found Mr Evans pressing his best trousers.

"Good evenin', Inspector – mind you don't knock over them flowers." He hastily saved the jam jar full of primroses and put it on the mantelpiece. "They was sent to me by a friend."

"Mrs Lube?"

The Miller meant to be ironical. He was staggered when Mr Evans nodded.

"We're goin' into partnership, me an' Old Sam," he said calmly. "The man's got his points but, as Amelia says – "

"Who's Amelia?" demanded the baffled detective.

"Mrs Lube – we're like brothers and sisters."

The detective looked at him suspiciously.

"What's the idea?" he demanded.

"Education an' combinations," said Evans profoundly.

"Let's keep the conversation clean," said The Miller.

And then Evans explained. It was, he said (untruthfully) his own idea. By some curious workings of chance, which even The Miller had observed, it fell out that luck balanced up and down. When Old Sam's Midnight Special was successful, Evans was unsuccessful. When Evans' fortune hit the beam, gloom reigned in the house of Lube. Why not therefore conclude a secret arrangement? Both parties to work independent one of the other and to pool profits. In this way, the misfortune of Old Sam would be relieved by the swelling coffers of Educated Evans. On the other hand, when the fickle goddess has deserted Evans, his exchequer would be supplied from the surplusses which came from his rival.

"Umph!" said The Miller. "That won't work!"

Mr Evans could afford to smile.

"As a matter of fact it's workin'," he said simply. "We've both had a good week, but he's had a better than me an' sent me four pun' six an' ninepence difference."

It appeared that Mrs Lube was keeping the books, that Mrs Lube's cousin was acting as accountant, and Mrs Lube's sister-in-law was preparing the balance sheet, and the money was to be kept in Mrs Lube's bank.

"It's a hundred to one against you, Evans," said The Miller ominously. Evans smiled again.

If it was not to be registered, the partnership was to be a very high-class affair. It was Mr Evans who suggested the telegraphic address, 'Evanlube, London', and in his enthusiasm paid the three guineas required by the postal authorities. "Not," said Mrs Lube, "that it makes much difference, for all the telegrams we shall ever get." Still, it gave the firm an importance when added to Old Sam's flamboyant notehead with a rubber stamp.

The week that followed was a tragic one for the followers of Educated Evans. He gave four £5 Specials that failed to finish in the first nine. His unbeatable cert for Friday – widely circularized – was a non-runner. On Saturday he called at the Lube household confidently, for Old Sam had had a wonderful run, including two 100-8 winners.

There was no accident about this except the fluke of Alfred finding Tom Dewbring, watcher of horses at Carshott. It happened that the three trainers at Carshott were enjoying the fruits of their industry and cunning, and sending out winners almost every day.

Evans knocked at the door with a gay heart and was admitted. Mrs Lube received him in the parlour and her manner was distinctly cold as Evans' was distinctly genial.

"I've had a tem'ry setback in fortune," he said breezily. "As dear old Hamlet said, you can't win all the time."

He produced from his trousers pocket a very small bundle of treasury notes, mostly, as Mrs Lube saw with a discriminating eye, green.

"Two pun' six," he said cheerily, and placed it on the table.

Mrs Lube's lips tightened. With some reluctance she produced her books.

"That's seven pun' five I've got to pay you," she said ungraciously. "What with all this money goin' out an' none comin' in and five mouths to fill, the instalment on the pianner due next week, I dunno, I'm sure."

What she did not know she did not specify.

"I got something up me sleeve for Tuesday, Amelia," said Evans darkly as he pocketed his money.

"Something that could fall down, get up an' then win. I had it from the boy that does him – a girl named Jackson who's keepin' company – "

"I dunno, I'm sure," said Mrs Lube again, and with those cryptic words dismissed the partner in her new business.

On the following Tuesday Evans started badly. He sent out Bollybill 'tried 21 lbs better than Coronach,' and Bollybill finished a bad last. On the Wednesday he pleaded with all clients new and old to go for Snatcher. 'This horse' – to quote his own words – 'is a Rod in Pickle. He's been brought over specially from Ireland for a coop.' Snatcher was seventh in a field of eight. On the Thursday The Miller met Evans at the entrance of Bayham Mews.

"I've just headed off a small deputation that was calling on you. I don't know whether I oughtn't to have pinched them for conspiring to murder."

Evans smiled tolerantly.

"What's one man's meat," he said, "is another man's poison, which is French for chickens. My dear old partner Sam has brought home two eight-to-one shots. Next week it'll be my turn. Mr Challoner, I got a horse for you on Saturday. He's a stone pinch. I had her from the boy – "

"If I were you," interrupted The Miller gently, "I should lose that boy."

On the Thursday afternoon Mrs Lube made up her mind. The telegraphic address was expunged from the notehead, and a postcard sent to the local post office informing the official in charge that 'Evanlube' might in the future indicate Evans, but it did not indicate Lube.

"Nobody sends us telegrams," explained Amelia to her husband, "except Mr Dewbring, and he puts our full name and address."

"What are you going to do?" asked Alf.

Mrs Lube smiled unpleasantly.

On the Friday afternoon she came to Myra Gray Mansions, and there was something very determined in her mien.

"Good afternoon, Amelia," began Evans. "You're just in time for a little bit of education. Take astronomy or the heavens – "

"We've had enough 'eavens, educated an' uneducated," said Mrs Lube, "and I'll thank you not to call me Amelia. Me husband objects. How have you done?"

Too well she knew how Evans had done.

"I don't suppose I've took a couple of pounds," said Evans cheerfully, "but luck will turn – "

"So will worms," said Mrs Lube. "You don't think me an' my poor dear gran'father's going to keep you in idleness an' losing our connection what we've built up through information *v*. gaswork?"

"Here, hold hard," said Evans, stung to annoyance by this gross plagiarism.

"You don't suppose," Mrs Lube went on, "that we're goin' to put your measly two pounds to our fifty day after day an' week after week an' year after year an' keep you in the bread of idleness with five mouths to fill an' my poor dear gran'father gettin' older every day?"

"Who ain't?" asked Evans loudly. "That's the evolution of nature, as I've told you till I'm sick of telling you. It's due to the subcutaneous tissues and bones – "

"Never mind about bones," said Mrs Lube, even more loudly. "You'll soon be gnawin' them if this goes on."

She planked a piece of paper on the table.

"There's five pounds – that's your share, and the partnership's over. We're not goin' to be ruined by educated has-beens and whatnots."

Evans turned pale with fury.

"You come to me for education – " he began.

"And we got it," said Mrs Lube. "The partnership's over."

Evans watched the departure of the lady from the top of the steps, walked back with a shrug, and applied himself to the task of composition.

That night, from information received, there was delivered by hand, or posted, to all clients old and new an important statement.

Educated Evans is once more Educated Evans.
Partnership with Uneducated People dissolved
and Abolished.

Educated Evans, the World's Premier Turf Profit and Adviser to the Nobility (by request) begs to announce that he has taken away his valuable advice from the so-called Old Sam (lately assistant and messenger boy to the well known Educated Evans) and now henceforward and herewith is on his own. Clients new and old who have received Educated Evans' beauties, can now have a horse that he's been keeping up his sleeve till he'd dropped all his low connections.

WET WHITE!
WET WHITE!
WET WHITE!

All clients new and old are advised to have their limit on this unbeatable gem, especially kept up the sleeve of Educated Evans. No connection with any other business, no longer adviser to Old Sam.

Great minds think alike. That evening Mrs Lube was turning the handle of a rotary machine which announced to the world that:

We have dismissed our assistant tipster, E Evans, having no use for same.

"Do you think," asked Alfred Lube thoughtfully, as they sat at breakfast and read Mr Evans' flamboyant claim, "do you think he's got anything up his sleeve?'

"His sleeve?" scoffed the infrequent partner of his joys. "He's had nothing up his sleeve, not even a shirt!"

Yet Wet White won; and on the Monday, at a Midland meeting, Too Gladly won at 100-6 and was Evans' special three-star help-yourself selection. And on the Tuesday Wiggletoe won, and was Evans' confident and unbeatable gem. And on the Wednesday up popped Small Schweppe in a two-year-old seller. Popped was hardly the word, since he exploded at the brilliant price of 20's.

Mrs Lube put on her hat and went out to interview Evans.

"Fair's fair all the world over, Mr Evans," was her opening. "Me an' my dear gran'father have got the idea that we've been a bit hasty – "

And then she stopped. On the table was a telegraph envelope addressed to 'E Evans, Esq., Myra Gray Mansions, Bayham Mews.' And by its side was a telegram, but the address was different: it was simply 'Evanlube London.' Slowly there dawned upon the good lady the horrible revelation. She had transferred the telegraphic address without realizing that she had been receiving Evanlube wires all the time!

She seized the telegraph form and read:

Blinkeye certainty tomorrow – Dewbring.

"A gentleman at Carshott," said Evans. "He's been sending me winners all the week. I don't know why. What was you saying, Mrs What's-yer-name?"

But Mrs What's-yer-name was speechless.

THE OTHER LUBESES

Educated Evans, being by nature gallant and by predisposition romantic, imagined, in the purity of his mind and the loftiness of his soul, that he might do almost anything that would be reprehensible in other men.

A lesser man might have thought twice before taking Millie Ropes to Lingfield. Millie was a little on the notorious side. She had left the bar of the White Cow with suspicious suddenness. There was a lot of vague talk about marked half-crowns. And she had subsequently disappeared from London, returning at the end of six months with a very small baby that she said belonged to her sister Annie, who had to leave England for Australia. Millie Robes was frankly an indiscretion on Evans' part.

"It's all over Camden Town, is it?" he said defiantly to a well-meaning friend. "Well, is it all over Camden Town that I give Orbindos – fear Melon – nothin' else mentioned? Is it all over Camden Town that I give Funny Freak – 100-6 beat a head – hard lines? Is it all over Camden Town that I give Priory Park before the entries come out? I don't take no notice of what common people say about us. I'm like the well-known an' highly respected King Edward the Professor, who picked up a lady's garter an' shoved it round his neck, hence the celebrated sayin' 'Hony swar kwee maly pense.' "

But Millie was not the only brick that Mr Evans dropped. Was he not seen at the Rialto Cinema with Mrs Alf Ibbidino? And was not Lou Ibbidino – her husband was in the ice cream business – a lady about whom the tongue of gossip wagged slanderously?

"She's a Satisfied Client of mine," protested Evans when The Miller reproached him. "What was I to do when she asked me to come to the films?... I *know* she's Livin' Apart... I know all about the barman at the Green Moon...but, Mr Challoner, I'm like the famous wife of Julius Caesar, the well-known King of Italy, I'm never suspicious."

Too well was Educated Evans doing for the Lubes to ignore this opportunity. Old Sam's Midnight Special announced:

OLD SAM

(*The Moral Tipster*)
83 years old and never got anybody into trouble.
Patronise the Man who Gave Myra Gray.
Old Sam gives tips that children can read.
Don't Support Vice, support purity.

Evans complained bitterly about this – his chief complaint being that Myra Gray was a figment of Lubean imagination.

But after a while the reflection upon his character began to get on his nerves. People began to stop him in the street and ask him not to speak to their wives. A woman who occupied a room in the mews told him he ought to be ashamed of himself – a man of his age. And behind it all was the crude propaganda of the Lubeses – apocryphal stories related to the hushed denizens of the bars by Alf Lube, scandal proclaimed over the tea table by Mrs Lube. Even Old Sam, that patriarchal man, made insulting references to the moral probity of the educated man.

"You've got to live it down," said The Miller.

"Live what down?" wailed the agitated Evans. "I done nothing – me character's bein' demobbed by them Lubeses and if I don't take 'em into court my name's not Evans!"

One day business took him to a foreign land – Camberwell, SE. He had to interview a friend who had settled in this strange country. This friend had a wife whose sister was walking out with the brother of a head lad in a Wiltshire stable, and the possibility of obtaining direct stable information was not to be missed. They had completed their business, and it had been arranged that anything the wife's sister told the wife about what her young man's brother had told her young man should be communicated by the husband to Evans at the earliest possible moment. And after Evans had told his friend to ask his wife to tell her sister to ask her young man to tell his brother that Evans paid heavily for news, the party was adjourning when he received a very staggering piece of information.

"I wonder, Mr Evans," said his friend, "whether you know of a job for my sister-in-law? She's been offered a place up your way, but she wants a little extra work to keep her going. She's as nice a young woman…"

Evans listened with closed eyes, framing the while a polite regret that he could not furnish the necessary employment.

"I've got meself into too much trouble lately owin' to bein' kind to wimmin," he said, shaking his head. "There's a certain party in Camden Town who's cast more aspiration on my character than the far-famed Lewdcreature Burgia, the well-known female Crippen of Italy. But I might hear of something – what's the lady's name?"

His friend gave it, and the educated man staggered.

"What?" he said incredulously. "Goo' lor'!"

His brain worked rapidly.

"I'll engage her," he said excitedly. "Five pun' a week if she'll come and do a bit of racing with me."

"She's highly respectable," warned the friend.

"So am I," said Evans.

Thereafter life ran with greater smoothness at Orbindos Manse – which, despite the ecclesiastical and evangelical character of the title, was the one room above a garage in Bayham Mews which was the *pied à terre* of the World's Turf Adviser.

Prosperity was revealed in the two flowerpots topped with the blazing blue of hyacinths, in the gold lettering on the door and, in the new green and magenta tablecloth.

"Good heavens!" said The Miller, stopping in the doorway to survey the unexpected grandeur.

Evans smirked in a self-deprecatory way.

"I got a young lady who comes in an' does," he said simply.

"Does what?"

Evans shrugged.

"Does for me. I got no time nowadays to go messin' about makin' beds and fryin' sausages."

The Miller turned the straw between his teeth.

"Attractive?" he asked.

Evans' shoulders went up and down.

"I scarcely notice the girl," he said indifferently. "Her name's Mrs Lube – "

"Eh?" The Miller's eyes opened. "Not your hated rival – and you let her come here?"

"She don't have any truck with Old Sam," said Evans, avoiding the visitor's eye. "As dear old B— Mary said to Cardinal Rishloo, the famous French poet, when she had her uncle chopped in four pieces for encouragin' Lady Jane Graves, 'Relations are best apart.'"

The Miller nodded slowly.

"I think you're mad!" he said.

"I'm quite 'in sansitas,' to use a foreign expression," said Evans calmly. "As a matter of fact she ain't any relation at all. But her name's Mrs Lube and she's partially a widder – her husband havin' run away with another lady. I pay her a fiver a week an' she's worth it."

News travels fast in Camden Town. Alf Lube, supporting the bar of the Grey Squirrel, heard a whisper.

"Here, what's that?" he demanded.

"He's goin' about with Mrs Lube – that's all I know. He was down at Kempton – or was it Plumpton? – with her. Harry Gribble, the bookmaker, said Evans introduced her in a gentlemanly way an' took seventy-five shillin's to five Cat's Eyes an' drew."

Alf went purple.

"That's a lie!" he said. "And for tuppence I'd give you a punch on the nose."

His informant laid two pennies on the counter and uttered truculent words. Apparently Alf neither saw nor heard. He dashed back to the headquarters of Old Sam's Midnight Special.

"Here!" he demanded wrathfully. "What's all this about you an' Evans? Here's me workin' me brains out an' tryin' to think winners an' you galivantin'…"

After he had picked himself up and Mrs Lube had thrown the broken chair into the scullery – she always used a chair as a weapon in her more distraught moments – "I'll go an' see Evans," she said, and went in search of her shopping bag. It was the only bag she had in which she could carry a poker.

Evans was not in when she bounced into his room. There was in his place a neat little woman in a flowered dress.

"Where's that…?" Mrs Lube described the educated man vividly.

"Moderate your language," said the calm guardian of Evans' home. "I'm a respectable woman an' not used to common talk. What's more, I don't want to lose me temper and slosh you one."

Mrs Lube gasped as an idea flashed on her.

"What name do you call yourself?" she demanded.

"Lube," said Mrs Lube II. "I call myself that because it was me husband's."

Mrs Lube I stood petrified.

"Your real name…no relation to me?"

"Gawd forbid!" said Mrs Lube II.

Mrs Lube staggered down the stairs a broken woman. Half a dozen broadcasters spread the tidings. So it *was* true…

People who scarcely knew Alf Lube came up to him and gripped his hand sympathetically. Perfect strangers offered him beer, and women came to their front doors to see him pass, shake their heads sorrowfully and say "Poor feller!"

As to Emma – which was one of her Christian names, the other being Amelia – she explained the matter to her husband.

"Another woman called Mrs Lube, eh?" he said, with cold politeness. "Oh, yes, I dessay…"

"Go an' see for yourself," hissed his partner.

Alf Lube said nothing, but looked murderous.

Detective-Inspector Challoner thought it necessary to warn his friend.

"Personally," he said, "I have no very strong feelings in the matter. We haven't had a good murder in Camden Town for years, and I should know who did it, because I happen to have heard that Alf Lube was trying to buy a German revolver that Joe Carter brought back with him."

Educated Evans turned pale.

"Is it my fault," he demanded, "that people talk about me for munce and munce, a scandalisin' an' deprecatin' me? As the well-known an' celebrated Cleopatra, her that hid Moses in the bulrushes said: 'You can't do nothin' if you can't prove nothin'."

"We shall see," said The Miller ominously.

He left Evans very thoughtful, though not for long. Mrs Lube II was a cheery soul, a lady of thirty-five; rather, as The Miller had supposed, attractive. She dressed neatly and took an intelligent interest in racing, so that Evans was more or less justified in adding to his circulars:

Address all communications and other postal orders to E. Evans, Orbindos Manse, or to my private secretary, MRS LUBE.

He had arranged to take her to Sandown. If the truth be told, Evans did not find his deception a very irksome one; Mrs Lube II was a presentable lady, who agreed with almost everything he said.

On the way to Sandown he explained to her the new move.

"You be my secretary, Mrs L," he said. "I'll give you another thirty shillings a week for that."

She brightened at the prospect; and there was room for improvement, for all that morning she had been glum and depressed – in fact, Mr Evans had the suspicion, when she arrived at the Manse, that she had been crying. She had had some bad news, she told him when he questioned her, but she made no attempt to inform him of its character.

"Naturally" – Evans pursued the topic as the train sped to Esher – "you haven't got my education. I don't suppose you ever will. Take the two seasons, flat and jumpin' – they're caused by the world going round on its axle or orbit. The farther you get away from the sun the colder it gets, which is natural, hence the National Hunt Committee an' the so-called sport of gentlemen. Take chemistry, botomy and syntax. Take mathematics or decimals. Take algebra, invented by the far-famed Euclid. Take hist'ry…"

Fortunately the train had reached Esher station before Mrs L. could take anything more than a passing interest in the scenery.

Evans had come down laden with information, but his star was not in the ascendant. There is no doubt that Guggs should have won the first race if he had been trying. But he wasn't trying.

"He ought to have won ten minutes," said Mr Evans hotly. "I had him from a friend of mine whose wife's sister is keeping company – "

Only then was he dimly aware of the presence of Alf Lube. The man was watching him evilly. When Evans walked into the paddock Lube followed, muttering incoherently.

"You're looking pale, Mr Evans," said Mrs L.

Evans smiled a sickly smile.

"I just remembered a client I didn't send Guggs to. We'll keep him, anyway!"

His unbeatable selection in the second race should have won pulling up, instead of which he was pulled up before he won.

"Tut, tut!" said Evans impatiently, as he glared through his glasses at the offending horse. "There's a bit of dirty work there."

He feared dirty work elsewhere; kept an apprehensive eye over his shoulder for Mr Alfred Lube. Never once did he miss his shadow. As Evans was standing by the ring marking his card, a hateful voice spoke at his elbow.

"You'll go on till you go off!" grated Alf Lube.

"I don't want any talk with you, my friend," said Evans loudly.

Lube laughed harshly. Later, Evans saw him in the bar, drinking whisky feverishly, and suggested to his companion that they should go home by the next train. But the fire of racing was in her and, on her disappearance into the ring to battle with bookmakers, Evans thought it was an excellent opportunity to explain the situation to the disgruntled husband of Mrs Lube I.

He saw him emerge from the bar, met his murderous scowl with a smile, and was about to approach him when his arm was caught in a firm grip and he was swung round.

The man who confronted him was six feet in height, and terribly broad. He had a strong, brutal face and light blue eyes that glinted murder.

"Here!" said the stranger. "I see you talkin' to a lady just now – Mrs Lube."

Evans opened his mouth but no sound came.

"She's my wife," said the giant fiercely. "I admit I done wrong, but a lovin' wife ought to take her husband back. When I see her this mornin' she wouldn't – someone's come between us. What is she to you?"

Mr Evans' mouth was dry, as the stranger urgently rocked him to and fro, and then inspiration came.

"Excuse me," said Evans, with what dignity he could summon. "I know nothing about the lady in question – she's a mere friend or client. I'm Educated Evans, the far-famed Turf Prophet. If you're Mr Lube then I have been mistaken an' I apologize. That's the gent who calls himself Mr Lube." He pointed at the glowering Alf.

Mr Lube II released his grip.

"Who – him?... Calls himself Mr Lube..."

Evans waited till the battle joined and sped blithely to the pass out gate. He did not even turn his head to see the result of the contest, but it was a satisfaction to him to see the ambulance speeding round the course towards Tattersall's.

MR EVANS PULLS OFF A REAL COOP

The Miller regarded his unfortunate friend with a stern but pitying eye.

"A tipster is a rogue until he starts backing his own wayward fancies," he said, "and then he qualifies for admission to the mug class."

Evans shifted uneasily under the other's gaze. "It was give me by the boy that does him," he pleaded. "This here horse was tried twenty-one pound and a beatin' better than Coronach. He could have fell down, get up an' *then* won. If he'd been trying – "

"It wasn't the jockey, it was the judge," said The Miller gently. "If *he'd* been trying hard he might have seen your unbeatable gem. But he's only human, Evans – he couldn't see so far down the course. Evans, I think you'd better stick to cars."

Evans ignored this insulting reference to a certain licence he held, he sighed and then, with a start of alarm, saw The Miller take from his pocket a hateful green paper.

"What them Lubeses say don't mean nothing to me," he said loudly. "Mrs Lube is no better than a lady ought to be. Old Sam's Midnight Special!" he sneered. "It ought to be called 'The Lodger's Moonlight Sonata'. She's worse than the far-famed Kate Webster that cut up her mother an' put her in a biscuit box. She's as two faced as the well-known weathercock on St. Pancases Church. That woman would take away a man's character an' never think twice about it. She's – "

"Leave the poor woman alone: listen and weep," said The Miller as he read:

Who sent three horses for one race?
>   EVANS!

Did they win?
>   NO!

Was they placed?
>   NO!

Is that education?
>   YES!

Stick to Old Sam who only sends one winner and that wins.

"That's what I call vulgar," said Evans hotly. "I wouldn't have that woman's disposition for ten million pounds. Education! Ain't I the only man that could ever ask Datas a question that could never be answered? Didn't I stand up for two hours and twenty-five minutes in Hyde Park one Sunday night and argue about drink till a policeman come an' moved me away? I don't mind Old Sam – he's not right in his head; but this here Mrs Lube, I'm going to bring an action in the High Court an' I'm consultin' me solicitor this mornin'. I wouldn't be surprised if she didn't get ten years."

Yet, for all Mr Evans' righteous indignation, there can be no question whatever that he had fallen into grievous error over the Stanborough Handicap. For, having sent out overnight Waxy, he had received information by the first post which induced him to change his selection to Fair Lady, and at the eleventh hour, as the result of an urgent communication which had come to him from the sister of a girl who had got into serious trouble with a head lad, he wired all his important clients that Funny Harry was walking over for that same race. And, as The Miller rightly and properly said, not one of those horses had finished in the first three, or, for the matter of that, in the first five.

Now a man may make mistakes and be forgiven. It was not the first time that Mr Evans had had the misfortune to tip more horses than one in a race; but on all these occasions Camden Town had forgiven him and offered him one more chance. But whether it was due to the wide publicity which 'them Lubeses' gave to his unfortunate mistake, or whether for some more esoteric reason, Educated Evans encountered a stone wall of hostility, and within three days of his *faux pas*, his clientele had been reduced to three persons, one of whom suffered chronically from delirium tremens. The other two never paid, so they didn't count.

Evans for once was sensitive to popular disapprobation. He sought vainly to justify himself, made a rapid circuit of his houses of call, was frozen out of three and physically thrown out of the fourth. Misfortunes never come singly; and it was Mr Evans' misfortune that he had ventured not only his reserve but his very rent money on Funny Harry, and it was a ruined man who pored over the evening newspaper, hoping that some misprint or a chance prick in the programme would act as a revelation from heaven and furnish him with the necessary means of rehabilitation.

Tragic indeed is the lot of him who, falling from a high estate of which he was the admired darling, discovers himself lying in the mud, a door-mat, on which the unworthy feet of sometime clients might be wiped, a gibe for Lubeses of both sexes.

Mr Evans felt his position acutely during those seven tragic days which followed.

If he could only have persuaded one of the old reliables to come back and act honourable, he might have mounted again to his former eminence; but with a unanimity which was terrifying, Camden Town refused to recognize the genius and integrity of him who had once been its pride.

He buttonholed Mr Harriboy, the eminent fishmonger and poulterer.

"I've got a horse in the Lingfield Plate – " he began.

"Keep it there," said Mr Harriboy roughly, disengaging himself. "He'll feel lonely without his two pals, won't he? You usually send three, don't you, Evans?"

"All I want to say to you, Mr Harriboy," pleaded Evans; but long before he could frame his justification and apology, Mr Harriboy has disappeared into the fish mortuary which he called a shop.

He tried with the landlord of the White Hart over a friendly whisky and soda which he could ill afford, and at that hour of the morning he could hardly digest.

"I got one for the Lingfield Plate, Mr Long," he said confidentially. "It was sent me in a curious way."

"I dessay," said Mr Long, wiping the counter mechanically. "And I expect you'll send it out in a curious way, but I'm not going to back it in any way. A man who sends one horse I can stand, but a man who sends three − and I got 'em all − is a man I never want to see in my house."

By the end of the day all Camden Town knew that Mr Evans had something unbeatable, something remarkable, something that could fall down, get up and then win the Lingfield Plate. Men told each other this fact with a quiet, sneering smile. It is true there were one or two weaklings who were almost inclined to subscribe, but the scorn and contempt of their fellows made them change their minds.

In perfect justice to these hard-shelled gentlemen, it must be confessed that Mr Evans had no unbeatable selection for the Lingfield Plate; he had hardly looked at the entries. Yet, in a mysterious way, his fate was bound up with three young men who were very greatly interested in a horse entered for that affair, and by the strange workings of Providence he was brought in touch with them.

It was evening and rather sultry. A heavy shower had fallen on Camden Town, making the roads greasy. He was walking along Hampstead Road when he saw a big car coming at a little above regulation speed in the direction of the West End. It tried to pass a taxi, skidded, did a graceful *chassé* towards the pavement, hit a lamp-post and, in some miraculous fashion came to a stop by the kerb without having sustained any greater damage than a smashed wing.

Before the crowd gathered, Evans went up to the window, and the first thing he realized was that the young man who was sitting at the steering wheel was slightly the better for drink. He was very cheerful, very talkative and in fact was screaming with laughter, as at a great joke, when Evans approached. His companions were a little better, or a little worse, according to the view you take of intemperance.

Now, if Evans had never driven a car, he had driven a van; and in his pride and skill he had managed to acquire for himself a driver's licence. He saw at some distance an approaching policeman; and whatever you might say about Mr Evans, you must admit that his mind worked quickly.

He opened the door of the car and got in, uninvited.

"Hi, what are you doing? Get out!" said the driver.

"You're right!" hissed Evans. "And if that flattie comes up you'll be pinched."

The driver was not so unsober that he did not recognize the truth of this unknown intruder's prediction. In an instant he made way, and by the time the policeman came up, groping in the region of his pants for a pocketbook, Evans was sitting nonchalantly at the wheel.

Happily the young constable did not recognise him and, after taking the number of the car, examining Evans' licence – which he had with him – and carefully examining the lamp-post, he allowed the car to proceed.

"Where are you going?" asked Evans starting the car with a grind of gears that set the occupants' teeth on edge, and certainly did much to sober them.

"We're going to St Jamesh Street," said the young man, who was now thoroughly alert. "And I'm most obliged to you," he said, after the exchange had been made. "Come along and have a drink."

In the palatial flat of Sir Henry Llewellyn Creen – for this proved to be the name of the driver – Mr Evans explained his vocation. He did not notice the three men look at one another significantly, and if he had he would have thought nothing more than that they were impressed by this chance meeting with one whose name was famous throughout the north-west district of London.

In the course of time he was dismissed, with a £10 note which he twice refused – until he was quite sure they weren't trying to take a rise out of him. The three young gentlemen sat round a table and discussed the great event of the morrow.

They were all fairly well off, and one of them owned a certain horse, Dictonite, a maiden four-year-old that had run six times as a two and had never been placed, had run not at all as a three, but as a four-year-old had been got ready for the Lingfield High-Weight Plate. It had not only been got ready, but every substantial bookmaker in the United Kingdom had also shared in the process.

There was in course of preparation amongst these young men the most colossal coup of the year. The race was to be run at 2.20 p.m., and at 2.15 p.m. one thousand two hundred and seventy telegrams were to be handed in at fifty post offices in various parts of England. They had borrowed names and they themselves had opened accounts wherever accounts could be opened; and their secret had been so jealously guarded that nobody, with the exception of their trainer and their trainer's head lad, was aware that Dictonite was 'walking' the Lingfield Plate.

They did not need the money, but they wanted the fun, and the organization of the coup had occupied three months which otherwise would have been spent in evading boredom.

They talked of Dictonite over a bottle, and then they talked of Evans over another bottle; at the third bottle they got back to Dictonite. And then the young baronet, who was the head of this lively gang, rose unsteadily to his feet.

"Boys," he said thickly, "we'll do this bird Evans a turn! Le's go roun' and see him and tell him to send out Dictonite to all his pals."

And they were in that state of mind that none of them recognized that the carefully laid plans of three months were on the point of going assy-tassy.

It was late at night when they clambered into a taxi, and a quarter of an hour later, after considerable search, Evans' flat was located, and they were thundering on the door.

Evans rose hastily and admitted his visitors.

" 'Slike this, ole feller," said Sir Henry gravely. "You're a goo' chap, we're goo' chaps. You're a tipshter, we're tipshters. You shend out Dictonite tomorrow morning...money for nothin', old thing...got many clients?"

"Fourteen thousand seven hundred and fifty-one," said Evans wearily.

"You shend Dictonite, old cock…"

"You'd better go home," said Evans, whose first thought when he had seen them was that they had called for the return of his £10 note.

"You shend Dictonite," said Sir Henry Llewellyn Creen again, and with this piece of profound advice they took their leave, each having in his bosom the glow which comes to drunken men who have done somebody a good turn at their own expense.

But the morning brought recollection, repentance and something like dismay. The elder of the three dashed into Sir Henry's room and woke him.

"I say, we were awfully drunk last night, but did we go round to that damned tipster and tell him about Dictonite, or did I dream it?"

The youthful baronet rose and rubbed his hair. "Oh Lord. We did, you know!" he said. "Wake up, Winkie, we'll have to have a council of war."

Winkie, the youngest of the three, was dragged from his bed, through to consciousness with a cold, wet flannel thrust into his face, and pushed into a chair at the council board.

"We must have been mad," said the penitent leader.

"What on earth can we do?"

"I'll tell you," said his second-in-command. "Let's send this bird a wire asking him to keep his mouth shut and not to send the horse, and we'll give him the odds to a pony."

The telegram was sent over the telephone, and three gloomy young conspirators went to their baths and bathed and dressed.

"If this feller sends the tip, it'll cost us about twenty thousand quid," said Sir Henry Llewellyn Creen, over his meagre breakfast. "Let's go and see him."

They went in a body to Bayham Mews, but no response came to their knocking. A taxi-driver, about to venture forth with his vehicle, volunteered the information that Evans had left early.

"I see him comin' down the stairs as the telegraph boy arrived – "

"Did he get the telegram?" asked Sir Henry eagerly. "Thank heaven for that!"

They drove to Lingfield with a lighter heart.

Evans had received the telegram. If the truth be told, he had left early in order to avoid an interview with his rapacious landlord, to whom he owed four weeks' rent. He had met the boy, had taken the telegram from him and thrust it into his pocket. It was his practice to receive, three mornings a week, a telegram from his correspondent at Lambourn; but as the last four he had from that quarter demanded payment for past work, he had got into the habit of leaving such messages unopened.

He had a yesterday's railway ticket for Lingfield which he had scrounged from a disgruntled backer who had succeeded in evading the collector and, after chewing off the date, he made his way to Victoria and eventually reached the course. Only very few intimates know how Mr Evans succeeded in reaching Tattersall's. He had three methods, and none of them had ever failed.

He was leaning disconsolately over the rails, watching the horses go down to the post, when he heard The Miller's voice.

"Had a bet, Evans?" asked Inspector Arbuthnot Challoner.

Evans smiled wanly.

"I got a horse in this race that couldn't lose," he said. "Pinpoint – help yourself. You can't put me off it. Three young swells came round to my flat last night and tried to stuff me with a horse called Dictonite – "

"Dictonite?"

The Miller looked at his card, then consulted his book of form, then shook his head.

"Not an earthly," agreed Evans. "That horse couldn't win a race – "

He stopped here. The field had started on its homeward journey. He had not even trouble to examine the colours of Dictonite, so that when the brown and purple jacket went past the post two lengths ahead of its fellows, he was under the impression that it was something of Jack Jarvis'.

"This horse Dictonite – " he began.

"It won," said The Miller.

"Did it?" said Evans, aghast. "Bless my heart an' soul. An' to think I had that horse give me by the owner. Tut tut! When your luck's out you can do nothin' right. Now I've got one for the next race, Mr Miller – "

But The Miller didn't wait to hear.

Evans strolled disconsolately into the paddock. He heard, with a shudder, that Dictonite had started at 100-6.

"What a nearly beauty!" he moaned.

And then he saw approaching him the young man whom he had displaced at the wheel on the previous night. The young gentleman beckoned him aside and Evans went.

"Did you send this horse out?"

It was on the tip of Evans' tongue to enumerate the number of clients to whom this gem had been sent, but second thoughts were best.

"To tell you the truth, sir, I didn't," he said.

"I gathered you didn't, from the price," said Sir Henry cheerfully.

He dived his hand into his pocket, produced a wad of notes and thrust them into the palsied hand of the World's Champion.

"Here are the odds to a pony each way, as I promised you in my telegram. Good fellow!"

He patted Evans paternally on the back. Evans held on to the railings with one hand and to the banknotes with the other. It was not until the numbers went up for the last race that he was sufficiently recovered to make his way to the railway station.

And that night all Camden Town knew that, though they had rejected the priceless information which Mr Evans had been prepared to give them, he himself had packed up a parcel. For did he not stand at the bar of the White Hart that night and pay for his drink with a £10 note which he stripped from a thick bundle of the same denomination?

THE NICE-MINDED GIRL

There is no doubt at all that Mr Nobbs, the celebrated trainer, was hot; and less doubt that Mr Snazzivitz, his chief and principal patron, was even hotter. Mr Snazzivitz was so hot that when he went for an insurance on his new cabinet works at Bethnal Green, the insurance manager sent for the police.

They were both hot and patient, and that made them even warmer. Mr Nobbs was quite content to run a horse down the course one day a week for the whole of the season, and pop him up at Warwick at 100-7 in the last week; the identical animal having finished tailed off last time out. And he felt no shame when he read in the morning newspapers that his horse had made every yard of the running and had been well backed.

There were many people who thought Mr Nobbs would be better off in another world, and bitter statements were made about the purblindness of stewards; but Mr Nobbs was never warned off, for he had an explanation up one sleeve and an alibi up the other and the only time he was ever called before the local stewards, he told such a pathetic and plausible story that there was some talk of raising a subscription for him, though it came to nothing.

It was the privilege of Educated Evans, the World's Premier Prophet and Turf Adviser, to know the barber who cut Mr Snazzivitz's hair whenever he was in London. And whenever one of Mr Snazzivitz's horses was on the job, the fact was whispered into the barber's shell-like ear for his own information and guidance, repeated to Educated Evans, and by him circulated the wide world over. So it might be said that the confidence of Mr Snazzivitz was only partially respected.

One afternoon Mr Snazzivitz met his trainer, the eminent Mr Nobbs, at lunch, and Mr Nobbs was both querulous and accusative.

"We ought to have got twenty to one about that horse yesterday, Snazzivitz," he said. "I didn't have a penny on him on the course; I told nobody, and even the stable lads didn't know he was going to run; and yet money started rolling in for him ten minutes before the off. Five to two's no good for me!"

"It doesn't fill me with the wildest enthusiasm," agreed Snazzivitz. "It must be that so-and-so barber of mine. I heard only this morning that he's a dead pal of that so-and-so Evans, the Camden Town tipster."

"Change your barber," suggested Nobbs.

"I know a better way than that," said Snazzivitz, an unholy smile on a large and cherubic face that was sprinkled with large and prominent features.

"They've spoilt one of the best coups we've ever had, and I'm not going to let 'em down as lightly as that. I'm the sort of man, Nobbs," he went on, "that never forget a friend or forgives an enemy. I'd work my fingers to the bone to help them that help me, and to destroy them that did me down. That's the kind of man I am!"

Mr Nobbs knew the kind of man he was without being told. He was the kind of man who, if you sent him in the ring to back a horse for you, returned you the starting price and pouched the difference; for Mr Snazzivitz was so rich that he couldn't afford to be honest.

Educated Evans occasionally employed female labour. He had not been very fortunate in his selections, it is true, but such was his faith in human nature, and so high was his regard for the female of the species that he never entirely lost hope. So there came to be installed at Forseti House the beauteous Miss Mary Rose, who was fair and slim and had wonderful blue eyes and fine, black eyebrows – all of which were attached to a body of singular attraction, so far as could be seen; and as she always wore the latest fashions, quite a lot was visible.

She was the niece of Mr Rose, the grocer, who was a great admirer of Educated Evans, and dreamed dreams of giving over the sordid cheese and butter business and embarking on the romantic adventure of an s.p. book. And since she was likely to be the only person he would trust, he was desirous that she should become acquainted with the peculiar technology of the racing world. And he had another reason for getting her out of the house.

"I trust her with you, Evans," he said, "and I wouldn't trust her with anybody else. She's a nice-minded girl, high-spirited and all that sort of thing, and she was brought up in a convent."

"With the monks," nodded Evans.

"I don't know nothing about monks," said the cheese man. "But she knows practically nothing of the world, and I want you to stand between her and, so to speak, temptation. I know you're all right, because no girl would look twice at you without laughing: you've got such a good-natured face," he added, and the ruffled Evans was hardly appeased.

He was enunciating his philosophy one morning, what time she folded with nimble fingers the announcements which were to gladden the hearts of all clients new and old.

"I daresay, Miss Rose," said Evans, "that I sort of puzzle you at times. Not that you ain't well educated, but you haven't got my experience and savvy fair, to use a foreign expression. I daresay sometimes you don't follow my reason and logic, but you'll get used to me in time, Miss Rose. I'm like the well-known William the Silent, the highly-celebrated Emperor of Germany; I don't talk unless I have to."

"Education is a wonderful thing," sighed the young lady. "I often wish I'd gone on to the sixth form."

"It's wonderful and it's not," admitted Evans modestly. "You get a bit fed up with people pointing you out in the streets and saying 'That's him!' But you've got to put up with that. The way they come to me to settle bets is getting a public nuisance. Do you know the date of the Great Fire of London?" he asked, closing his eyes and raising his eyebrows.

She shook her head.

"No, I'm only twenty-one," she said. "I don't quite remember; it must have happened when I was a baby."

"Sixteen-forty-three," said Evans rapidly, "during the reign of the great Queen Anne, known as the virgin queen because of her friendship for the great Duke of Marlborough, the ancestor of Winston Churchill. The last time the Thames was froze over was in fourteen-seventy-two, the year we defeated the Germans at the Battle of Trafalgar Square – see Lord Nelson."

"I wish I knew as much as you," said Mary Rose wistfully.

"You can't," said Evans. "It's not given to everybody. It's a gift, the same as a voice for singing purposes. All my work is brain work. I've got to carry things in me head tha'd drive you silly! When did Eclipse win the Derby?"

"Last week?" she hazarded, having only a vague knowledge of the sport of kings.

"Eighteen-seventy-two," said Evans with even greater rapidity. "It was run during a snow-storm and Jack Jarvis, the celebrated trainer put a ball of butter in the horse's hoofs so that he'd slide round Tattenham Corner. Eclipse was the half-brother to Bayardo, from which the mighty Bart Snowball is descended. See Stud Book!"

His further lesson in ancient history was interrupted by a tap at the door. Evans himself opened it and saw a resplendent gentleman smoking a large cigar and wearing what appeared to be the entire contents of Sam Isaacs' jewellery store.

"Name of Evans?" he asked.

"Yes, I am Mr Evans," admitted the educational authority.

The newcomer swept the room with a glance in which contempt, amusement, resentment and disgust were unskilfully blended.

"I'd like to have a word with you when you're alone," he said.

Evans looked at the young lady, raised his eyebrows with great significance – he had very flexible eyebrows – and she took a hasty departure.

"Now, Mr Evans." Mr Snazzivitz sat down uninvited on the only comfortable chair in the room. "You've probably heard of me. My name is Isidore Snazzivitz."

"The celebrated owner?" asked Evans, interested. "Who trains with the well-known Mr Nobbs on the far-famed Berkshire Downs?"

"That's me," said Snazzivitz. "You've been sending out a horse of mine. I'd like to know where you got your information."

Evans knit his brow.

"I send out so many horses," he said. "Perhaps, if you'll kindly name the animal – "

He paused enquiringly.

"Bluebottle," said Mr Snazzivitz, and a look of intelligence came to Mr Evans' already intelligent face.

"Bluebottle? I seem to remember the name…yes, yes, I sent it out on my five-pound special. I had it from one of my touts."

"You had it from my barber – that's who you had it from," said Snazzivitz unpleasantly. And then, remembering his mission, he forced a smile to his face. "Now look here, Evans, you're not a bad fellow; I've heard a lot about you; and if you ever want a tip, come straight to me. Don't go messing about with my barber. I'll tell you anything I know and anything that's going. Here's my address" – he produced a large card with a floral decoration in the corner – "I live only ten minutes' walk away," he said. "Never hesitate to come and see me, and maybe I'll put you on to one or two good things. You're interfering with my business, Evans, and that's a fact. What chance have I of getting a job home when you're circulating it round Camden Town? You see what I mean?"

Evans saw what he meant. Such condescension from a real owner was most overpowering. He could only bow.

"That's a very nice girl you've got. Where did you get her?"

"She's a friend of mine," said Evans, with a certain amount of dignity. "I never give away the names of the staff."

Now Snazzivitz had come with no other idea than to take a firm grip of a possible cause of annoyance, for he had many horses due to win and, so to speak, his winter's keep was looming ahead. And it was vitally necessary that no so-and-so tipster should send his so-and-so horses – as he himself tersely described the situation – and spoil his something-o-other market. Which was a feeling very right and natural, and held in common with other speculative owners, trainers, jockeys and jockeys' valets. But he was a susceptible man, and the sight of those blue eyes and that rose-and-milk complexion, that svelte form and other appendages peculiar to radiant femininity, shifted, so to speak, his angle of vision.

The next morning he called again. Evans saw him coming down the mews and uttered a few words of warning and admonition to his assistant.

"You want to be careful about that man," he said. "I'm so to speak responsible for you to your uncle. Ever heard about the gipsy's warning? I'll get you a copy this afternoon. If he asks you to go and have a bit of dinner with him, just be 'aughty – like that!" Evans gave an imitation of a haughty young lady of twenty-one.

"I wouldn't dream of going," said the girl. "Who is he?"

"His name is Snazzivitz," said Evans rapidly, for the man was coming up the stairs. "He's a horse-owner and a rooey."

"What's that?" she asked, in open-eyed wonder.

"A man that doesn't know when to stop," said Evans.

"Backs horses. But the bookmakers are getting wise," said Evans, "and they're closing his accounts. He used to have about four hundred, but they're shut down now, and he's always on the look-out for mugs to open accounts for him."

"How perfectly dreadful!" said Mary.

It was perfectly true that Mr Snazzivitz was that kind of man. He was the greatest job merchant of his year, and when he wanted to back a horse he not only used his own accounts, but he had a large list of friends who, for a consideration, would lend their names and accounts for his purpose. Thus, if you are John Jones and have an account with Macpherson the eminent bookmaker, you could by arrangement lend him a wire addressed to your bookmaker, and at the psychological moment he would back the horse for £5, the odds to £1 being yours, the odds to £4 being his; and if the horse went down, which it never did, he would refund you the £4 you had lost.

"Does he get a lot of money that way?" she asked wistfully.

"Packets," said Evans.

"How wonderful!" breathed the girl. "I mean, how dreadful to take it perhaps from the poor bookmakers and to deprive them as it were of sustenance for their wives and shoes for their little children! I wonder he can sleep at nights."

"I don't know that he does," said Evans.

And then Snazzivitz came in.

"Talking about horses," he said, his eyes on the peerless Mary, "I've had a tip for one that's going at – er – er – er Lingfield on Saturday, a horse called Head."

He did not take his eyes from the girl. Evans was annoyed. He was annoyed because there was no meeting at Lingfield on Saturday, and because Head had already won there.

"Good morning," said Snazzivitz. He was not speaking to Evans.

The girl raised her timid eyes from her work and dropped them again.

"That's a funny job you've got," said Snazzivitz in his most amiable tone. "We shall have to improve on that, eh, Evans?"

"This is my business," said Evans loudly, "and I'd be obliged if you didn't speak to the clurks."

A look passed between the two. Evans, unused to the artfulness of courtship, saw nothing. Did she scribble '8 o'clock, Cobden Statue' on her blotting pad? If she did, she scribbled it out again, because he could see nothing but wriggly lines when he examined the pad later. At any rate, Mr Snazzivitz did not prolong his stay.

He was a youngish man, and people who wanted to be in his good books, or men and women of defective vision, might describe him as handsome. Mr Evans, returning from the Bull and Crow after a heated argument with Mr Lube on the ethics of tipping, had occasion to walk through Mornington Crescent, a somewhat deserted residential thoroughfare; and there he had the shock of his life. A man and a girl were walking in front of him, arm in arm, their heads together, their pace leisurely. Evans gasped.

"Good God!" he breathed.

He had a good mind to go back and challenge Mr Snazzivitz, reprimand the girl, wave her dramatically in the direction of the grocers, and send her home. But he did not.

The next morning, when he went to his office, Miss Mary Rose was not there. Instead was a little note in which she said that she found the work was rather heavier than she had expected, and with her uncle's permission she had decided that a woman's place was at home.

"Education's wasted on that girl," said Evans bitterly to The Miller at the first opportunity. "That man's no better than the celebrated Looey the Nineteenth who used to chase nimps through the glades of Fountingblue. I'm going straight to her uncle."

"I shouldn't if I were you," said The Miller. "That young lady can take care of herself."

"She went to a convent – " began Evans.

"She was also chucked out of the convent for teaching the younger students the game of banker," said The Miller.

"But her uncle sent her to me because – "

"Her uncle sent her to you," said The Miller patiently, "because she tossed the errand boy for his salary with a two-headed ha'penny. If you can teach her anything, you might send the subject along to me, will you? That girl will do anything for money except work."

Yet she was a good girl, as she told the discomfited Mr Snazzivitz, when he offered her almost everything in the world, except a marriage certificate, to share his life and fortune.

"I will do almost anything for you, Ronald," she said, with sweet childish impetuosity, "and haven't I already opened twenty-five accounts for you in dear uncle's name? At least, on dear uncle's notepaper? And there'll be another thirty by tonight's post. You can't ask me to do more than that."

"I love you – " began Snazzivitz.

"I know, and I love you dreadfully," said the girl, shaking her head, a tear trembling on her eyelashes. "But we must be sensible, mustn't we? I don't even mind being married at a registrar's office; you can always get the photographers there, and I make an awfully good photograph. But this idea of a Bloomsbury flat is so dreadfully vulgar and shocking that I cannot let myself think about it."

Mr Snazzivitz was content to wait. They dined that night at the Laurence in Wardour Street, and they supped that night at the Boolum Club, and they lunched next day at the Empress Club, and went to tea at the Regent Palace, and dined at the Worlingham – in fact they were quite a lot together. And all the time one of Mr Nobbs' charges, a noble animal called Button Boots, was nearing perfection.

On the night before the Hurst Park meeting Mr Nobbs came up to London and saw Mr Snazzivitz.

"This horse," he said, "could pull a bus and win. You haven't been to that so-and-so barber of yours, have you?"

"I'll so-and-so watch it!" said Snazzivitz luridly.

"Then we ought to get 100 to 7 for our money. Have you opened any new accounts?"

Snazzivitz nodded.

"A friend of mine has opened sixty," he said complacently.

The next morning The Miller met Mr Evans and made a suggestion.

"Button Boots?" said Evans dubiously. "He hasn't been placed all the year, and he's been running in selling plates! You don't expect him to win a good-class race?"

"There's a whisper round the town."

Evans smiled sourly.

"That Snazzivitz couldn't win a race," he said definitely. "He won't have no luck for the rest of the year. He's a kidnapper, a snake in the grass and a rooey! I'd like to do him a bad turn, but – "

When The Miller had gone, Evans sat down to consider the matter. He had no very definite views on the race. Why not send out Button Boots, if only to annoy the man for whom he had conceived such a deadly hatred? To think, with Evans, was to act. To all clients new and old the message went forth.

SIR, Have a good win on
BUTTON BOOTS
This horse has been tried to be 21 lbs. in front of the highly celebrated Pickaboon. Help yourself, and don't forget your old friend Educated Evans.

And Button Boots won – at a modest price, it is true. For there was an illusion in Camden Town that Evans knew all about Nobbs' horses, and his fame as an informant in the matter of these animals had spread to the very end of the world, which is somewhere beyond Croydon.

He was reckoning the possible revenues from his success when the door was flung violently open and the innocent girl came in. Her eyes were blazing, her cheeks were white.

"Did you send out Button Boots?" she hissed.

"Yes, Miss Mary," said Evans, rising with politeness. He was always a gentleman.

"Then what in hell do you mean by spoiling my market?" she howled at him.

She left Evans staggering and dazed. As she turned out of the mews she was met by Snazzivitz.

"Oh, here you are!" he said, relieved. "You got those wires away? It was a rotten price – I don't know why – but so far as I can make out, you'll be sending me a thousand pounds on Monday – "

"A thousand buck-rabbits!" said the blue-eyed child with startling malignity. "It ought to have been three thousand if that pie-faced mutt had closed his big mouth! And listen, Mr Snazzivitz, I'm English, and my motto is 'What I've got I hold.' If you ever got any money from me, book the address – I'll be writing from a high-class lunatic asylum!"

THE MUSICAL TIP

It is a curious fact, that must have impressed itself upon the observant, that people who move in an environment of splendour seldom realize their own good fortune.

For example: there are men and women who live at those earthly paradises, Blackpool and Southend, all the year round and are unconscious of the blessing. There are coarse stage hands who see beautiful actresses every day of their lives and are oblivious to their beauty. Similarly, Sir Boski Takerlit knew and entertained some of the wisest trainers that were ever licensed by the Jockey Club, and yet profited not by so much as a penny from the priceless information which came his way.

"Rubbish and nonsense!" he used to say of racing.

"The man that backs horses is a stupid ass – hein?"

How he came to know these trainers at all is a long story but may be briefly condensed. He was an authority on the musical comedy and operatic world, and when he wanted to put a girl in a small part his recommendation was almost a command. And there were many naughty trainers who, quite unknown to their wives, were interested in furthering the stage ambitions of pretty young ladies in whom they took more than a fatherly interest.

Lady Takerlit was not so well known to all who go racing as, say Old Kate. In fact, for certain reasons she never went racing at all, because, to her husband, racing was anathema. He was a popular musician and had been knighted. It is a well-known fact that any man who wags a baton before a hired orchestra playing somebody else's music simply can't escape being knighted. Round about New Year's Day the Flying Squad scour London to find a conductor who isn't a Sir and, clubbing him into insensibility, they tie a Garter round his neck, hit him on the head with a sword and his name henceforth is Sir Mud.

Sir Boski Takerlit was a rich man, having recomposed several popular tunes of the last century. Her ladyship – as she was often called – was a democrat. That is to say, she was happiest when she was in the company of her intellectual and social inferiors. They were sometimes difficult to find, for this is the truth: Sir Boski, in a moment of temporary insanity or spiritual exaltation – one is sometimes mistaken for the other – married his housemaid. She was pretty and once upon a time had been slight. She was still pretty when, an optimistic circular having come her way, she wrote to Educated Evans.

> DEAR SIR,
> Please send me your 5 pound special. I enclose po for 2s 6d.
>> Yours Truly,
> > LADY TAKERLIT.

She always signed herself 'Lady Takerlit.' Otherwise, as she said to her husband: "How the hell would they know I was a lady?"

Mr Evans sent his £5 Special for 2s 6d. The usual price was 5s, but he never returned money. And the horse he sent was a winner.

> Thank you, dear Evons! (*she wrote.*) I backed Marked Marble and as you say. What a beauty! Pray pop round one day to tea. The buttler will show you in.
> > Yours truly,
> > LADY TAKERLIT.

She usually referred to her buttler in such letters.

Evans popped round to Micklesfield Square. He was met on the doorstep by Sir Boski Takerlit, who glared at him.

"Who the blazes are you?" asked Sir Boski.

"Mr Evans, of Masked Marvel Mansions," said the educated man; "commonly known as the World's Champion Turf Adviser – "

"Tipster!" roared Sir Boski. "So it is you that has let my wife astray! Ged oudt!"

Evans got oudt.

He did not know that Sir Boski was both jealous and mean. This he learnt later when her ladyship called on him one dark evening.

"I don't really know how I can look you in the face, Mr Evons," she said. "I don't reely! The way my husband went on to you is simply disgraceful and disgusting."

She looked round the little room; to her it seemed agreeably cosy, for in truth she was rather overawed by the magnificent Victorian surroundings in which she moved.

"Good idea having your office over a stable – I suppose you keep your horses downstairs?" she said.

Evans inclined his head gravely, though in truth the only animal beneath him was the provision merchant's Ford van.

"You've no idea how near he is, Mr Evons, and him with money to burn and everything. If I didn't make a bit of pin money now and again I don't know where I'd be. But don't send me any more – he opens my letters. I'll pop round and see you, and now and again I'll be able to give you a tip."

"My ladyship," said Evans, with old-world courtesy, "the pleasure will be yours."

He kissed her hand. He had seen pictures of people kissing the hand of royalty and he thought it was the right thing to do. Unfortunately, at that second the door was opened and Bogey Jones appeared. He had come to borrow the *Sporting Chronicle*. It was an embarrassing moment, but Evans, quick-witted, thought of an expedient to get rid of the visitor: he had reason to regret his intelligence.

"Them that acts honourable *is* honourable!" said Educated Evans emphatically. "An' them that *don't* act honourable would pinch the nails out of a orphan's boots an' sell 'em to blind men for cloves!"

"Which, reduced to the language of Camden Town, means that you've been had," said The Miller unsympathetically. "Anyway you're a Can – nobody but a Can would trust Bogey Jones."

"I don't know what you mean by Can, Mr Challoner," said Evans with dignity "I've never got hold of the low talk that abounds or percerlates through Camden Town. Bogey is a tea-leaf: we all know that, but tea-leafs act honourable in their sportin' transactions – see Palmer, the well-known Rugby doctor who poisoned his bookmaker rather than knock him."

"Rugeley," murmured The Miller.

"Wherever it was. Bogey Jones is a Twister. If he ever gets married he'll have a family of corkscrews."

"Perhaps he'll return the money," suggested The Miller.

Evans made a noise like a meditative duck.

"As the well-known W Shakespeare said to Lord What's-his–name – him that got his napper cut off for takin' a liberty with Queen Elizabeth, the so-called Vergers Queen because she used to go to church so often – "

He paused, having missed the path.

"Shakespeare," prompted The Miller.

"…As he said one day when him an' David Garrick the well-known artist who painted Lady Godiva, her that did the bare-back ride down Coventry Street to advertise the Back Ache pills – "

He reached a crossroad.

"Shakespeare," murmured The Miller.

"As Shakespeare said – you can't expect nothin' from a pig but a grunt."

Evans took out the stump of a cigar, sneered at it and put it back in his face.

"I'll get Bogey," he said.

"In the meantime you've been got," said The Miller gently, "and it's your own fault."

Inspector Challoner reproved him. "Imagine a man like you, as wide as Broad Street, giving Bogey a five-pound note and asking him to bring you the change in the morning. It's inexplicable!"

The Miller had a line of classy words of four and five syllables that was the admiration of High Street, Camden Town.

"It may be ines-what you said," retorted Evans hotly, "but the money's gone."

The Miller frowned and eyed him curiously.

"There is something at the back of this act of guileless trust on your part," he said. "A woman!"

Evans went red and spluttered.

"A woman!"

"A lady!" protested Evans passionately. "A lady of title an' as pure as a driven snowball! If you want to know – "

"I don't – " The Miller's manner was pointed. "Scandal has never interested me."

Evans looked round as though he expected to discover an army of secret service agents waiting to note his words.

"I gave that fiver to Bogey, to Save a Woman's Name."

"And you got no change," said the practical officer. "I don't think that you came off very well."

Evans shrugged his shoulders.

"It was the Price I Paid for Honour," he said mysteriously.

The Miller was thoroughly interested.

"If you'll stop talking like an old melodrama and get right down to solid earth, I'll give you a round of applause," he said.

But Mr Evans smiled cryptically.

"Aristocracy," he said simply.

Evans learned by accident that her ladyship had been ordered by her indignant husband to close her two modest bookmakers' accounts – the accounts were modest, not the bookmakers – and then one night there came to him a mysterious message.

Dear Mr Evons,

I must tell you somethink of great importonce. My husband will be out tonight conducting his orkystra. Expect me about 10.

Yours truly,

Lady Takerlit.

PS. Don't let anybody come popping in after I pop in.

At ten o'clock that night a mysterious figure might have been seen flitting into Bayham Mews. It was not seen as a matter of fact, because it was a rainy night and nobody was particularly interested even in mysterious figures. But Evans waited at the top of the stairs. The light was shaded in his room, and he experienced all the agreeable sensations of a conspirator.

Her ladyship mounted the stairs cautiously, as she had become a woman of weight, and panted into Evans' office in an agitated state. Evans closed the door – the curtains were already pulled – and then he took the covering off the light.

"Oh, Mr Evons" – she was on the verge of tears – "I feel I've got to speak to a Man about his Goings On! I'll divorce him, Mr Evons! I won't be trod on like a worm. I've stood it long enough."

"It's a long worm that has no turning," said Evans seriously. "What has his lordship been doing, my ladyship?"

She sat down breathlessly on a chair, and as breathlessly related the story of a letter, discovered by accident, as all such letters are discovered, while she was searching his pockets for papers of a greater monetary value.

"I'll divorce him before the Lord Chief Justice his own self!" said her ladyship tremulously. "He's a low, common Hungarian from Austria, and I bemeaned myself by marrying him! I'll get almony out of him, too. This comes of his mixing up with low, common chorus-girls. All musical people are alike, Mr Evons: they don't know where to stop, and even if they do, they don't."

Evans listened gravely, shook his head, uttered tut-tuts of surprise and horror; and when she had exhausted her denunciations of musical genius, she unburdened her soul on a matter which was much more important.

"I told you I'd give you a tip, Mr Evons, and I will," she added vehemently. "We had one of them – those, I mean: forgive me being unladylike – trainers up to lunch today, and whether Boski's told 'em or not I don't know, but they never speak about horses in front of me. But I did hear something." She nodded more emphatically than ever. "It's going to win at Newbury. It's the biggest certainty of the year. In fact, Mr Evons," she said, "this horse can't lose. You never heard of a horse like that?"

Evans had heard of horses like that, and had frequently described them in his optimistic circulars.

"Did you hear the name, my ladyship?" he asked.

She shook her head.

"No, that's where the – where my husband was artful. The only thing I know is this" – she spoke slowly and deliberately – "the horse runs on Wednesday and the name of the horse is the name of a piece he's playing as an extra on Tuesday night at the Albert 'All – Hall, I mean; I'm so upset that I don't know even how to speak grammar. That's what Boski said when they whispered it to him."

"It'll be on the programme," said Evans thoughtfully.

She shook her head.

"No, they never put the names of the extras on the programme, but it'll be after the third piece is played. He's bound to get an encore, and then he'll play this other piece. It's operatic – that'll all I know."

Evans considered.

"The Merry Widder?" he said.

She didn't think it was the Merry Widder.

" 'I'll take you back if you want to come back'?" suggested Evans, going rapidly through his repertory.

"Is there a horse called that?" she asked.

Evans had to admit there wasn't.

"We'll easily find out. Go to the hall the night before, and anybody will tell you what it is. And, Mr Evons, will you put a ten-pound note on for me?"

She produced the ten-pound note. Evans waved it aside and continued waving until she showed an inclination to replace the money in her bag. He stopped it halfway.

"I'll learn him!" said her ladyship, quivering with annoyance.

In this vague and altogether unsatisfactory way did Educated Evans become possessed of the gem of the year.

She left him in a very studious mood. She was going to divorce her husband; and her ladyship had looked kindly upon him. There was an understanding between them...

Evans walked to the wall and looked into the four square inches of cracked mirror. He wasn't bad looking, he confessed: he was on the right side of fifty, and he was a man of fame and education.

The next day he sounded The Miller as to the propriety of marrying a divorcée.

"Not that I'm a marrying man," he said, "and as for titles – bah!" He snapped his fingers. "I don't want to marry just for the sake of being Lord Evans..."

The Miller explained gently that marrying a knight's lost lady would not entitle Mr Evans to a seat in the House of Lords.

"Wouldn't it?" The educated man was obviously disappointed.

"I suppose," said The Miller, "you thought it would look fine on the circulars.

"LORD EDUCATED EVANS
The World's Champion Turf Prophet.
Address all money orders c/o the Lord Chancellor.

"But it can't be done."

Evans shrugged.

"I'm a socialist meself," he said, "practically red."

He did not tell his friend anything about the musical horse. Indeed, he kept his secret locked in his own narrow chest; for secrets have a habit of leaking out, and the Lubeses sent forth from day to day crowds of spies and informers to discover and anticipate the substance of Evans' £5 Specials.

Classical music was Greek to Mr Evans; and naturally he was not particularly well versed in operatic selections. He looked up the newspaper, saw that Sir Boski Takerlit was conducting the New Brighton Symphony Orchestra, but the programme told him nothing. He had never heard of a horse called 'Three Dances from Henry VIII', nor did he know of any animal who answered to the name of 'Rachmaninoff's Prelude'. He settled himself down to prepare for the great coup, got out his circular complete, leaving only a space into which he would insert, by means of a rubber stamp, the name of this unparalleled quadruped.

The Miller met him when, arrayed for the evening, with his pockets stuffed with handbills advertising his virtues as a finder of winners – for, as Evans argued, you never know what business might be brought in by a few bills dropped judiciously in a public place – and wearing the famous plaid trousers and gold pin, he sallied forth to an evening's entertainment.

"Music?" said The Miller incredulously. "I didn't know you had any tastes in that direction – or are you going to take a peep at the injured husband?"

"I'm going to get a little information," said Evans mysteriously. "And as for music, it's education, ain't it? The well-known and highly respected Mozart who wrote the Moonlight Sonata – "

But The Miller had passed on.

Evans found the Albert Hall crowded when he arrived and, with great reluctance, paid for his seat.

"If you *are* Press," said the manager, "I'll admit you, but what paper do you represent?"

"I won't argue," said Evans loftily. "What's the cheapest seat you've got? For two pins I wouldn't go in and report your music at all."

Eventually he found a seat at five shillings on the floor of the house, and made his way in with a look of disparagement on his face. He was fortunate enough to get an aisle seat in a row half-way between back and front, and for an hour he listened uncomprehendingly to a succession of musical acrobatics. Standing on a little platform in front of his orchestra was Sir Boski Takerlit, whom he recognized instantly.

"A bit of showing off, ain't it?" he asked his neighbour, an aesthetic young man with horn-rimmed glasses. "Him standing up there so that everybody can see him?"

The young man was startled and made no reply.

"It's what I call gettin' yourself in the limelight," said Evans, warming up on the subject. "It's pushin' yourself forward."

The young man maintained his silence but edged a little farther away from the companion which the booking-office had thrust upon him.

"It only shows what a dirty dog he is," said Evans. "He don't play nothin', he simply stands up there an' chucks his arms about, and when people clap he starts bowing an' scraping as if he did it all."

"I don't wish to speak with you," said the young man in a very elegant voice.

The applause that greeted the third piece was deafening. Evans joined in, because he was anxious that the encore should be given.

There was no announcement: the piece started with a thunderous beating of drums. Evans in frantic anxiety turned to the studious young man.

"What's the name of this bit?" he asked.

The young gentleman ignored his insistence.

"Do you mind tellin' me what's the name of this song they're playing of?" quavered Evans.

The young man turned in a fury.

"If you don't leave me alone I'll send for an attendant and have you turned out," he said.

People were scowling at the educated man and twisting their necks round and glaring at him, in the way typical of all music-lovers. Evans began to perspire.

Eight hundred and four envelopes, all addressed and all stamped. Eight hundred and four circulars, ready to receive the imprint of this gem of the year. And what it was, heaven only knew!

And then a wild resolve came to him – an inspiration. He rose and walked swiftly along the aisle. Before him was a short flight of steps leading to the platform, and above this two more steps to the rostrum where Sir Boski, unconscious of the coming interruption, was waving his baton ecstatically. In a stride Evans was on the platform; in another, he was peering over the shoulder of the outraged conductor.

Low murmurs arose from the hall; a voice cried "Chuck him out". And then he saw the word on the top of the page…

Fortissimo!

With a chortle of triumph he turned as a red-faced attendant grabbed him by the collar and dragged him to the aisle. He had a dim vision of royal-looking personages surveying him with amused interest. And then another hand gripped him and he was dragged towards the door. One disengaged hand he thrust into his pocket, grabbed a bundle of handbills and flung them wide. A few seconds later he struck the pavement with a dull, sickening thud.

Mr Evans rose with a beatific smile, waved a cheery hand to the attendant, and shuffled off. The musician's secret was his!

The next evening The Miller came to see him.

"Yes, yes, I know Fortissimo won. But, you poor piece of cheese, Fortissimo isn't the name of a piece of music, it's a direction meaning 'louder'. Obviously the horse was Lohengrin – that was the piece they played. And Lohengrin was pipped on the post by a short head…Fortissimo!"

Evans closed his eyes and smiled.

"What a beauty, what a beauty!" he murmured. "Straight from the trumpet's mouth!"

PSYCHOLOGY AND THE TIPSTER

Mrs Lube had a cousin, a young man who had done well for himself. He was in fact an educated man and a school teacher, albeit with socialist leanings.

When the Lubeses talked of Cousin Arthur they did so in hushed tones. His portrait hung in every Lube parlour, including the parlour of that Lube who had been sent to Canada by the late Dr Barnardo.

Cousin Arthur very infrequently visited his relations, for he lived in a magnificent semi-detached villa at Streatham, but when he did he gave ample warning and the parlour was dusted, the table polished and a fire was lit. This latter being an important event for, as everybody knows, the fire is never lit in the parlour except on Christmas and Boxing Days.

He came after due notice and was received in the manner of a reigning prince paying a state visit to a feudal dependant. That is to say, Mrs Lube brought crumpets for tea and a bottle of Gilbey's port wine – the genteelest of all refreshments.

Arthur Stickleburn was a young man who wore horn-rimmed glasses, a red tie to proclaim his abhorrence of capital, and a large gold watch to emphasize his affluence. He had a ready smile, was affable to Mrs Lube, gravely respectful to Old Sam – who sat in a corner, his hands clasped over his stomach and his beery eyes glued to the bottle of port – and comradely to Mr Lube.

After they had thoroughly and exhaustively discussed all the relations who had died since they met last, and what sort of funerals they had had, Mrs Lube told him some of her troubles. And in the front rank of these was Educated Evans.

"And of all the perjurous hounds that ever lived, Arthur, – if you'll excuse my language - there's nobody like him. An' me strugglin' on with three mouths to feed, and his a bachelor, makin' money hand over fist an' gettin' winners…"

Cousin Arthur was amused.

"Educated, is he? In what direction – philosophy, science, archaeology, philology – ?"

None of these sounded familiar to Mrs Lube. She explained her difficulties.

"H'm! I seem to remember having heard of the fellow," mused Cousin Arthur, stroking his weak chin thoughtfully. "I wish I could spare the time to deal with this person. Educated! I don't suppose he has ever read a line of John Stuart Mill or heard of the Binomial Theorem."

"Whose horse is that?" asked Mrs Lube hopefully.

Cousin Arthur smiled.

"It is not a horse – it is a Calculus," he said, and then, after frowning consideration: "Psychology is what you want," he said. "Fortunately that is one of my strong points. Tell me something more of this man and I may get his Psychology."

Mrs Lube shook her head.

"You'd never get anything out of him," she said. "He's so mean, he uses his tea-leaves twice!"

Cousin Arthur explained, so far as she was able to comprehend, just what he meant. He elaborated his plan, grew enthusiastic with its growth.

A week later the news went forth to Camden Town of Mrs Lube's dire straits, and naturally Detective-Inspector Challoner, who was the repository of all fairy stories, came to learn of her domestic trials.

There comes to most men to whom fate has been unexpectedly kind, a large and growing sense of benevolence. Toby Walker, drawing fifty shillings from Issy Issyheim over a successful up-and-downer, enters the saloon bar of the Red Lion, nods genially to the assembled company, and the glad cry of "What's yours?" falls upon grateful ears. Mr Issy Issyheim, on his annual visit to Monte Carlo, struts forth from the Cercle Privée and throws a *mille* note to a chance acquaintance with a nod and a smile; one suspects M. Blanc, the guv'nor of the rooms, to disperse his doings in a similar glad spirit of munificence.

Educated Evans was in that mood which is so acceptable to the importunate ear-biter when the news of the Lubeses' misfortune came to him. He had sent out three winners in succession, and the majority of his satisfied clientele had acted honourable. With crinkling banknotes in his pouch and the peace of God in his heart, he strolled forth into the snowy wastes of High Street, Camden Town, reconciled even to the inevitable abandonment of the Windsor meeting. And opposite the Nag's Head, who should he pop up against but The Miller, a straw gripped between his teeth and his face a little redder than usual.

"Heard about Mrs Lube?" asked The Miller.

"I don't want to hear anything about them Lubeses, Mr Challoner," said Evans loftily. "They take the low road and I take the high, as the good book says, an' we never meet. Socially they're not in my set. As Rishloo, the celebrated French clergyman, said to Cardinal Valtaire when they was in France: '*Demi-tasse, demi-monde,*' which means that one half of the world don't know how the other half drinks and the other half don't care."

"She's ill," said The Miller, a little dazed by the erudition of his learned friend.

"Poomonica?" asked Evans, interested.

"No, not pneumonia – if that's what you mean – nervous breakdown. Old Sam's broke, and her husband's run away with the barmaid at the Cow and Garter."

"Not the red-haired one?" Evans was fascinated by the news.

"I don't know the colour of her hair," retorted The Miller impatiently. "But she is certainly – Mrs Lube I mean – down and out."

Evans made a faint tut-tutting noise.

"It had to be," he said complacently. "I kill all competition. Information *v.* gaswork. Knowin' *v.* pickin' 'm out with a pin. I got one that's runnin' on Tuesday that's past the post! Tryin' for the first time since last year's National. This horse is fourteen pound better than Ruddygore an' ten pound better than Silvo – an' he's in a seller! I got him from the boy who does him."

Mr Challoner's concern for the unhappy Mrs Lube momentarily evaporated.

"What's this – Ned Carver?" he asked, with provocative sarcasm.

"Ned Carver's gone to stud," said Evans, unperturbed by the implied scepticism. "So has Bart Snowball and Sergeant Murphy."

The Miller explained certain reasons why none of these horses was likely to make successful sires.

"It's a shame to treat horses like that," said Evans severely. "Anyway, this horse I'm tellin' you about is goin' for the coop of the year. You know Sarkles the trainer – he's hot! Whenever a horse of his wants a poultice he just leans against 'em."

"Sarkles? Then it's Bonny Whitelegs you're talking about?"

Evans wagged his head in annoyance.

"I ought to wear a muzzle," he said; "but you'll keep this to yourself, Mr Challoner? This is the biggest coop that ever looked through a saddle. Keep it quiet and we'll get eightses to our money."

The Miller made a mental note and reverted to the subject of Mrs Lube.

"Yes, I know that she's no friend of yours," he interrupted Evans' protest, "but she's a woman."

"So was Lewdcreature Burgia, the female Crippen," said Evans bitterly. "So was Cleopatra whose needle we all admire; so was B— Mary who done in the little princes in the well-known Tower by pourin' poison in their earholes! So was Catherine, the celebrated Queen of Russia, massacred all the inpatients of Bartholomew's Hospital because they wouldn't have any truck with the Hugenuts; so was Mrs Manning, who was hung in a blue silk dress at Horsemonger Lane Goal for murderin' her nine little children – see Dickens!"

He might at that moment wash his hands of the Lubeses, dismiss them to the outer oblivion, shrug them into the infinite spaces where wander The People Who Don't Count; but in the cosy comfort, not to say fug, of his office at Desert Chief House, and what time he smoked a good cigar before a blazing fire, the thought of his sick enemy came back to him and his conscience stirred uneasily.

On his new table were stacked five hundred and forty stamped, addressed envelopes. Into these shortly would be inserted the circular already printed, advertising the merits of Bonny Whitelegs. In his skyrocket a wad of notes rustled musically every time he crossed his legs. And in that dark and saddened home lay a woman deserted by the man to whom she had given her hand and confided her destiny.

Evans sighed. And then a formless thought took shape.

He went out into the chill night with a basket, and procured from Higg's, the grocers, a jar of invalid jelly, a dozen new-laid eggs, a packet of oatmeal and various other luxuries associated in his mind with the effective treatment of sickness.

In the kitchen of Mrs Lube's house sat Old Sam, Young Alf Lube and the partner of his joys and sorrows. Old Sam was asleep and, by the happy smile that transfigured the patriarchal face, it was easy to suppose that he was dreaming of strong drink.

"It's a bit rough on me," grumbled Alf Lube, "poked up in the house all day and night waitin' for Evans to come – a silly idea I call it."

Mrs Lube bridled.

"What about me?" she demanded. "Every time there's a knock at the door do I have to go into the parlour an' lay on the sofa or don't I? Answer me."

"Silly idea!" gloomed Alfred. "As if this Sy— whatever the word is – is goin' to bring Evans here. An' what about my reputation? Me supposed to have run away from you with a common barmaid!"

"You seem to bear up all right," she said.

"Do I? Suppose *she* gets to hear of it – what's she goin' to say?"

Mrs Lube stiffened.

"She – which 'she', I'd like to know?"

Alfred Lube was embarrassed.

"Well…whoever it is. I don't know her myself, never so much as said 'How d'ye do' to her. But she's got her feelin's, the same as the rest of us."

"Barmaids haven't got any feelin's," said Mrs Lube, her suspicious eyes on her husband. "You seem to think a lot about what she'll think, Alfred!"

He closed his eyes wearily.

"Whose idea was it – did I say anything about runnin' away with barmaids? Wasn't it your cousin Arthur with his Sy-something?"

"Don't speak a word about my cousin," she said with acerbity. "This sy-sausagy, or whatever it is, can't be wrong. He couldn't harbour a wrong thought."

"What's it mean?" demanded Mr Lube.

"Findin' out – it's a new way," said Mrs Lube, and at that moment there was a gentlemanly knock at the door.

It was opened to Evans by a small boy who wore a black tie. Evans thought for a moment that his purchases would be on his hands.

"Mother's ill," said the sepulchral child. "So's grandfa'r."

A husky voice from the parlour asked "Who is it?"

"Mr Evans, Mrs Lube," said the educated man loudly.

"Come in."

Mr Evans removed his hat reverently and tiptoed into the parlour. On a sofa drawn up by the fire lay Mrs Lube. She wore her oldest dress and there was a bandage round her head.

"Come in, do, Mr Evans," she moaned. "I suppose you've come to gloat over me?"

"Far be it from me to gloat," said the virtuous Evans, "but as an educated man it's me duty to do unto others as I'm done by. I've brought you a few things."

Mrs Lube glanced sideways at the articles which her visitor put upon the table, spreading them out so that none might escape her attention.

"Set down, Mr Evans – Willie, go out into the kitchen and don't make a row or I'll break your neck!"

Willie withdrew and slammed the door. Mr Evans sat on the edge of a chair, a look of condolence and sympathy on his face.

"We all ought to stand together," he said. "Misfortune, as the saying goes, makes cowards of us all. What's the matter with you, Mrs Lube?"

"Internal," she said.

Evans coughed and was silent. He was not a family man.

"I don't think I'm Here for Long," she added.

Evans made a noise expressing his sorrow.

"Well," he said, "we can't expect to live for ever. You've had your life – what are you, Mrs Lube, about forty-five?"

"Thirty-three!" she snarled. "What's the idea of forty-five?"

She mastered her emotion with an effort, but Evans was not put out.

"I suppose you get light-headed when you're ill," he said. "I remember you twenty years ago an' you was no chicken then. Anyway, you've had your life – we all have to go sooner or later. Lube's run away?"

She nodded: she could not trust herself to speak.

"I think it must be with the red-haired one," meditated Evans. "I always guessed there was something wrong ever since I saw 'em coming out of the cinema together."

Mrs Lube sat up suddenly.

"When was this?" she demanded fiercely.

"Must have been a month ago," said Evans. "But don't agitate yourself, Mrs Lube – after all, he's a younger man than you – "

"He's four years older!" she stormed.

"Men keep young longer than women," said Evans soothingly. "As the well-known Julius Caesar the Eyetalian said – "

"Never mind about *him*!" interrupted Mrs Lube. "You say you saw him with a barmaid at the cinema, do you – the dirty dog!"

"Set your mind on Heaven," said the educated man gently. "You know the worst, Mrs Lube. He's gone – forget him. Can I do anything for you?"

It was then that Mrs Lube remembered that she was being far too energetic for a person *in extremis*. She accordingly relaxed into her role of interesting invalid.

"No, Mr Evans, there is nothing you can do for me," she said faintly. "I'm sure I'm much obliged to you for the 'am – "

"Jelly," murmured Evans.

"You're very kind. Before I passed, as it were, I'd like to have sent out a winner – but what's the use? We're ruined, me an' my poor dear grandfather – no clients – no money for paper, no stamps – nothing. I don't want to sent it out, only just to know it."

Evans considered the matter deeply. Here was a woman, in a manner of speaking, on the very edge of Tophet. Basely deserted, starving, as it were, and wanting one gleam of sunshine which he was in a position to radiate. And yet –

"How's Old Sam?" he asked.

"Ill in bed – not expected to recover – business gone, Alf gone – everything gone," she wailed.

Evans took the plunge. Leaning over her, he hissed: "Bonny Whitelegs – help yourself an' tell the angels!"

She opened her eyes wide.

"Him?" she said doubtingly.

"Got it from the boy that does him – a lad called 'Orace – nex' Wednesday. Keep it to yourself, Mrs Lube, an' have a real good win. You ought to have a bit of money to leave to your children!"

Mrs Lube breathed deeply.

"Oh, if I could only believe that," she whispered, "I'd pass peaceful! You sendin' it out, Mr Evans?"

"Tuesday night – late," he said briskly. "Now don't leave it to him an' his carrotty girl, Mrs Lube. She's had enough from what I've heard. Three pun' ten he paid for the di'mond bracelet she was wearin' of when I see her last – *an'* the hat he bought her at Stibbinses!"

Mrs Lube was very pale; her eyelids fluttered furiously.

"Bracelet..." Her voice sounded strangled. Mr Evans thought the end was near. "Hat...three pun' ten!"

She's wandering, thought Evans, and tiptoed out of the room.

The door had hardly closed upon him when Mr Lube, smoking a cigarette before the kitchen fire, heard his wife's firm footfall in the passage. And then the door opened and she entered.

"Did you find out anything – " he began, and then he saw her face and, swift to move, dodged the jar of invalid jelly.

On the Thursday:

"Mrs Lube has made a good recovery," said The Miller.

Educated Evans looked at him pained – for the time being speechless.

"And Bonny Whitelegs – what a beauty!" said The Miller. "I had forty pound to five. And I presume that all clients old and news received this gem?"

Evans shook his head and found his voice.

"At three-thirty on the afternoon of Tuesday the fourteenth ult.," he began dreamily – and obviously it was a bad dream – "I was sittin' or reclinin' in my chair when I had a telegram – 'Don't send out Bonny Whitelegs. Horrace.' I ought to have known," he mused, "that it was a swindle or imposture, but me bein' what I am, I put it aside an' said 'Another day.' An' he won…an' the Lubeses sent it out to all clients new an' old. An' Alf Lube sent the wire from Marlborough because a friend of mine see him gettin' into the rattler at Paddin'ton with a black eye an' a lip as big as a cushion… my horse…!"

"Mrs Lube – " began The Miller.

"Is alive." Evans nodded gravely and pointed to the black armlet about his sleeve. "She's alive – ain't I in mournin'?"

THE SHOWING UP OF
EDUCATED EVANS

It was unfortunate that Mr Yevers, the landlord of the Cow and
Garter, loathed Educated Evans with a deadly loathing. Mr Yevers
himself was an uneducated man. At best he could only affix his name
to the south-east corner of a cheque with the very greatest labour. As
for reading, when anybody pointed out a paragraph in the newspaper
he invariably replied: "Read it out – I've mislaid me glasses."

His career had been a romantic one. Starting as a small boy,
penniless and friendless, he had worked his way up to be first the
barman and then the manager of the biggest house in North London.
And as this was in the days before the prevalence of the cash register,
Mr Yevers had diligently acquired sufficient money. With his savings
he purchased his master's business (when that gentleman went into
Carey Street as a result of his carelessness and the dishonesty of his
subordinates), and by the application of his industry and a little
fencing on the side, he attained to wealth beyond the dreams of
actresses.

He was a self-made man, and had nobody else to blame for it.

He hated Evans primarily because of his education, but particularly
because Evans, in an argumentative moment, had unconsciously
betrayed Yevers' shortcomings.

It was over the old vexed question as to when the Thames was
frozen last, and on what date a coach and four was driven across at
London Bridge.

"I remember it as a boy," said Yevers, who never would admit that anything happened before he was born.

"You're mistaken, sir," said Evans, courteously enough. "It was in 1452, in the reign of Good Queen Anne, the celebrated dead lady – "

"I remember it as a boy," asseverated Mr Yevers hotly.

"If you can read – " began Evans, meaning nothing ill.

Mr Yevers went a dark blue and pointed to the door of the saloon bar.

"Get out of my house before I kick you out!" he said.

And because great minds brood upon little things, Mr Yevers brooded upon the affront which had been offered him by a man who, as he rightly said, hadn't as much brass to his name as Mr Yevers took in the saloon bar in one evening.

"How was I to know he couldn't read or write?" protested Evans to The Miller. "The ignorance of the lower orders is simply remarkable and stupefying. I've no desire to hurt the man's feelings. He's a bung, an' I can't say anything worse to him than that."

"You've lost a client," said The Miller.

Evans smiled sardonically.

"Three times a year, and I have to take me winnings in beer, which is repugnant to me, being a gentlemanly spirit drinker. Or a bottle of port wine from the wood and made of it! I've wiped him off me books."

The Miller, the champion pacifier of Camden Town, succeeded in reconciling the ruffled Mr Yevers. Unfortunately for all concerned, the reconciliation coincided with a period when things were going badly with Yevers. He had in two new barmen and a sub-manager in a month. But such is the mechanical mind of the present generation that the seemingly insuperable difficulties presented by the cash register were overcome by all three of them, each in his own way. And then, in a moment of insanity, Mr Yevers decided to have a plunge on a horse whispered confidentially across the counter.

He went down to Lingfield to see the horse run; was genial, almost convivial until…

As the field came into the straight with Jiggling Jimmy ten lengths ahead, Mr Evans turned to his companion with a shrug.

"Information *v.* gaswork," he stated briefly. "Knowledge *v.* pickin' 'em out of a hat! As I told you, Mr Challoner, this here Jiggling Jimmy could fall down – "

"He has!" said The Miller.

Mr Evans opened his eyes and glared through his glasses.

"That ain't Jiggling Jimmy…yes, it is…no, it ain't…yes, it is."

"Shall I say 'when'?" asked the sympathetic Miller. "Tough luck, Evans!"

Tough luck it was, for Jiggling Jimmy, having fallen and dislodged his rider, was still leading the field as it passed the post.

Educated Evans threw his race-card on the asphalt of Tattersall's, jumped on it, lifted his nose in a bitter sneer, and sent his glasses back in his case with a crash; it was the gesture of a defeated warrior sheathing his sword.

"That horse was tried twenty-one pound better than Jerry M and two stone better than Tom Pinch," he began. "An' to think that – what did win it?" he asked suddenly.

"Cat's Eyes," replied The Miller, and Mr Evans breathed heavily through his nostrils.

"Old Sam's Three Star Nap!" he said hollowly. "Is that luck or ain't it? Was Cat's Eyes on the map? I'm asking you."

"I heard you," said The Miller, as they made their way towards the rattler. "It's sad – but it's racing, Evans. Such things happen."

Evans had forgotten all about Yevers' existence in the passionate despair of the moment, and when that blue-faced man confronted him on the platform he was dumbfounded by the injustice of the attack.

"Tipster!" he roared. "You bring me down here and make me have monkeys on horses that can't stand up on their own legs! Why, Old Sam's worth a million of you – two million," he amended generously.

In the face of such vulgarity Evans could merely shrug his shoulders.

"Speaking as an educated man – " he began.

"You're a fake!" howled Yevers, shaking his fist in the face of erudition. "You don't know nothing about nothing and never did!"

A most persistent patron of the Cow and Garter was Old Sam, and to him Yevers confided his woes in the condescending way which publicans have with their moister clients. Old Sam sighed and shook his head in his melancholy way.

"You'd better by half have stuck to me. What won the race, Mr Yevers?"

"Cat's Eyes."

"That's a good horse," nodded Sam soberly, though he wasn't. "As nice a horse as ever lived."

"You tipped it," said Mr Yevers.

Old Sam scratched his nose.

"Did I?" he said. There was a note of genuine surprise. "Why, of course I did! Bless my soul, I've give so many winners that I don't know what I tipped."

"As for his education – !" said Mr Yevers.

Sam smiled.

"He gets it out of a book," he said confidentially. "I know: he used to be a partner of mine. He gets it all out of a book. Not his ideas at all."

Now the idea of showing up Educated Evans might have gone no further but for the fact that Yevers was called away to a sick relation in a little country town; and as the man owed him a bit of money and, moreover, since there was no written acknowledgment of the debt – this was the principal cause of the anxiety – Yevers thought it advisable to call on his relation and secure from him an acknowledgment that at any rate his executors would honour...

This took time, because the sick man was also a very obstinate man, and one of the symptoms of his disease was an extraordinary lapse of memory, so that he could not recall any time when he had ever borrowed money.

The matter satisfactorily settled, Yevers found time hanging on his hands, and went into a small variety theatre. And there he saw on the stage the most charming young lady, who answered the most obstruse and difficult questions fired at her from the audience with an alacrity which almost suggested that she had some good friends in the audience. He asked the man on his right the name of the lady, and learnt that she was Liza, the Human Encyclopaedia; and later, having a drink at the bar with the manager, he learnt that Liza wasn't as successful as he would have expected her to be.

"It's out of date, that sort of turn," said the manager. "People aren't interested in ancient history any more."

An idea flashed through Mr Yevers' mind. He learnt the girl's salary, and interviewed her in a dressing-room and discovered to his joy that she had once graced the private bar of a high-class establishment in the West End.

He engaged her on the spot.

The Cow and Garter was not a House that was a particular favourite of Educated Evans, and even the arrival of Miss Betty, the new and even more gold-headed-than-usual barmaid, did not attract him, though the fame of her spread throughout Camden Town. For beauty, as Mr Evans remarked originally, is but skin deep and very often not that.

"What girls are comin' to nowadays, Mr Challoner, I can't understand," he said in despair.

"I wonder," mused The Miller, "if you are as good a judge of beauty as you are of horses? Because, if you are, I shouldn't like you to pick out a wife for *me!*"

Evans smiled tolerantly.

"Wimmin don't like me – I know too much about 'em. Take Hist'ry – "

"If you are going to talk about B— Mary..." expostulated The Miller.

"I ain't," Evans shrugged. "There's others, an' as the widely advertised Shakespeare says, 'I've learnt about wimmin from all of 'em!' Take the well-known – "

"Not Lewdcreature Burgia!" begged The Miller. "Let that poor lady rest in her marble tomb – "

"Lipsus lazily – not marble," corrected Evans. "She was buried in Westminster Abbey by the side of her dear old father in sixteen eighty-four – correct me if I'm wrong. Her last words was 'You'll find Callis engraved on me brain' – her end was peace."

The Miller fanned himself vigorously.

"No," Evans went on, "I'm referrin' more to such wimmin as – "

"Cleopatra," murmured The Miller, "whose needle we all admire!"

Mr Evans' annoyance was not wholly without cause.

"I'm thinkin' of wimmin like Bore-de-Syer, the well-known Roman queen that fought the ancient Britons in a chariot with mowin' machines tied on the spokes! What a woman!"

"Ah!" agreed The Miller densely. "A friend of yours?"

Educated Evans could only make impatient noises.

"Anyway, I don't get lured up to no public-houses by females," he said. "I got my reputation to lose."

"May I suggest," said The Miller, with infinite gentleness, "that you not only lose it, but that you tie a brick round its neck and drop it into the Regent's Canal. So that it doesn't come back. As to the new Circe – "

"Pardon?" said Evans.

"Temptress," amended The Miller, "her chief interest to me is her education. She's one of the best-read girls I've ever met and she has a memory like a loose-leaf ledger. I confess that she staggered me when she told me the date the police force was founded."

"Seventeen-forty-three," murmured Evans, "by the celebrated Lord Copper – it used to be Peel, I know," he added to The Miller's correction, "but he changed his name for family reasons."

"Her education," went on The Miller, "is rather remarkable. People are talking about it. Yevers says he had her schoolmaster in the saloon bar the other day and she fairly staggered him."

"Anything staggers a schoolmaster," scoffed Evans. "Besides, how can a bit of a girl be educated? Where's her experience? Where's her man-of-the-worldness? Take geography: diamonds come from Amsterdam – very few people know that. Sugar comes from

Demerare, coffee comes from Africa, cotton comes from Liverpool and dear old Dixieland – see song. Take mathematics – "

"Eh?" said The Miller.

"Take mathematics," said Evans calmly. "What about algebra? What about Euclid? What about isosceles triangles – that's geometry: you do it with a compass. I got a prize for it at school. Take physics. What makes a seidlitz powder go fizz? Very few people know that. It's the combustion of the blue with the white…"

Curiosity and tentative invitation extended at third hand, plus the fact that several people had told him about the young lady at the Cow and Garter, eventually induced Evans to make a call.

Yevers was standing in the bar, a sardonic smile upon his face, as Evans strolled in with a certain *hauteur*. To his surprise, the landlord came towards him.

"Let bygones be bygones, Evans," he said thickly. " 'Ave one on the 'ouse."

"Port wine," said Evans, "or maybe a glass of sherry white wine – as seck as possible. Seck's Latin for sweet, hence the word seckarine."

This was a challenge, delivered alike to the awe-struck habitués of the Cow and Garter, who had gathered to witness this Homeric contest, and to the beautiful lady who was regarding him with the speculative eye of a gladiator confronted with a large and unshaved lion. Yevers looked round at her and frowned significantly. Here was her quarry.

"Sherry," she said, in a clear, loud voice, "comes from Jerez, pronounced Hreth, in the south of Spain. 'Sec' means 'dry'. Sherry was first introduced into England in sixteen forty-two."

"Forty-one," murmured Evans. "The first lot was brought here by a gentleman named Williams." He was on the point of saying "a particular friend of mine," but checked himself in time.

He glanced round the saloon bar, stared insolently through the windows.

"Looks like snow," he said; "which reminds me that the Thames was froze over in seventeen-fourteen and a coach and six horses drove across at Wapping Stairs."

"The Thames was frozen over," said the belle of learning, "in seventeen-forty-two at Richmond Bridge, and a whole ox was roasted on the ice near Putney in eighteen-thirty-one."

"Thirty-two," murmured Evans; "and it wasn't a whole ox, it was half an ox. It was the year that Diomedes won the Derby."

He thought this would stagger her, but she was a girl not easily staggered.

"Diomedes," she said, "was a bay colt by Argos-Capdane. He was trained by H Leader and owned by Mr Beer. As a two-year-old – "

"I'm not talking about that Diomedes, there's another," said Evans loudly. "You've got 'em all mixed up. I'm talking about the horse that won the Derby in seventeen-eighty-four, owned by Lord What's-his-name and ridden by Fred Archer, the well-known but late jockey."

She was staggered by this, but came again nobly.

"Fred Archer was born – " she began.

"Everybody knows that," said Evans. "What about Socrates, the well-known poet and Eyetalian, the fellow that double-crossed the well-known Rubicons – him and Julius Caesar was like brothers. So was Mark Antony, the highly celebrated friend, Roman and countryman."

"Shakespeare – " she began.

"Never mind about Shakespeare," said Evans, holding tight to his vantage. "What about Brutus, that chewed tobacco?"

"Tobacco – " began the girl.

"Never mind about tobacco. Did he or didn't he? Didn't Julius Caesar, when he lay a-dyin' on his couch on the Plain of Nervy, say 'Et chew, Brutus?' Is that hist'ry or making it up? And what about Cleopatra, who was stoned to death by rats? What about her needle, which we all admire, covered over with hydrostatics, which I used to be able to read when I was a boy, as everybody knows, though I've got out of speaking Egyptian, though I still know a few words, such as 'ooka' and 'woohka' which means 'male' and 'female', as there is in every country throughout the British Commonwealth, on which the sun never sets. Which brings us to Australia. The finest horse that ever came out of Australia was Carbine, by Musket out of Woodbine. He ran in seventy-five races and was only beaten once, his jockey havin' a packet on the second. Take Flemington race-course, the finest course in the world, where the Viceroy's Cup's run. Which brings us to the question of Ireland."

Hebe made her supreme effort.

"Ireland was conquered by Richard Strongbow in ten sixty-six – "

"I know all about that," said Evans. "He landed in Galway 'Arbour on the thirteenth of July at seven o'clock in the morning. It was raining," he added. "Which brings us to the question of how many pennies put side by side would reach from here to the moon. Very few people know this. The moon is an extinct volcano, entirely surrounded by ether. Chloroform was invented by Dr Lister by accident whilst trying to discover the secret of gunpowder. In sixteen thirty-five: I am not sure of the exact date. Talking of doctors reminds us that Lewdcreature Burgia, the female Crippen of Italy, who poisoned the little princes and buried 'em under the stairs where the Marble Arch now stands, was one of the most educated women of the day. Her husband was the well-known Leonardo D Vincey, the celebrated picture-taker, whose portraits we all admire, both in the British Museum and otherwise. The British Museum was founded by an old sailor who wanted the people of London to have a place to go into when it was wet."

The female encyclopaedia lost her head.

"Look here, Mr Whatever-your-name-is," she said hotly, "all these dates and things you're giving us are wrong. You know they're wrong. And all my dates are right: I got them out of the Encyclopaedia of General Knowledge, and I learnt the two thousand pages by heart."

Evans smiled.

"I wrote it," he said simply.

THE SUBCONSCIOUS MIND

The eternal quest for education led Mr Evans into many strange experiences. There was a Cult that had meetings in a tiny hall in Stibbington Street and the educated man was for some time a regular attendant.

"What is this I hear about your going to the meetings of The Children of the Sun?" asked The Miller.

Mr Evans smiled.

"It's learnin'," he said simply. "I gotta subconscience."

"A what?" asked the startled officer.

"A subconscience — it's workin' all the time. It's due to the sun."

"But you never see the sun in Camden Town."

"I go racin'," said Evans. "When a man gets a subconscience he gets Revelations. Things come into his mind. It's in a book. Sometimes when I'm walkin' about I get a subconscience of what I'm going to have for dinner; sometimes I get a subconscience that I'm goin' to meet you. It's astral."

"Whatal?"

"Astral — somethin' to do with flyin'," said Mr Evans.

"Kite-flying?"

Evans smiled again indulgently.

The life of a prophet, even a world's champion prophet, is not all jam. He is at the mercy of temperament — temperamental horses, temperamental jockeys, and last, but by no means least, temperamental clients. No clients of Educated Evans better fitted this description that Moses Smike, the owner of Smike's Renowned Fish and Chip

Restaurant, whose establishment was off Great College Street, Camden Town.

And yet Evans had undoubtedly been the salvation of the man. As long ago as Braxted – what a beauty! – and Eton Boy – given from the weights some clients got 33-1 – he had encouraged Mr Smike in the pursuit of easy wealth. Only the other day, when Mr Smike had some difficulty with the wholesaler who supplied him with plaice and skate, it was the Educated Marvel who found him Obscotch (8-1) and Bunions (11-2), and thus rescued him from an appearance in the Bankruptcy Court.

"I wouldn't mind," complained Mr Evans, "if the man would say a thing an' stick to it. But when he says 'There's a tenner for you, Evans,' an' when I call for it there's only a middle piece and eight and threepence in coppers, I consider he's not acting honourable. And coppers is low – with all due respect to you, Mr Challoner, an' meanin' nothing against rozzers."

Detective-Inspector Challoner took no umbrage. He was in his most cheerful mood that morning, and the straw he chewed was whiter and more imposing than usual.

"Smike's going to be married," he said, and Evans uttered a tut-tut of surprise and disapproval.

"Why, he's an old man! It'll be like the celebrated Mr May marryin' the well-known Miss December!"

"To be exact, he is about your age," said The Miller. "Anyway, I shouldn't be surprised if he made amends by asking you to the wedding."

Evans brightened visibly.

"Perhaps he'll give me a weddin' present?" he said.

The Miller explained that the giving of wedding presents was the privilege rather of the guest than the host.

"That's a silly idea," said Educated Evans. "Anyway, the most he'll ever get from me is my Sealed Ten Pound Guarantee Coop wire – that's worth a dollar of anybody's money."

The bride was Miss Emily Jane Loocood and she was supposed to be of French origin. She had been an assistant at Mr Smike's fish establishment for six years.

"And about time he married her," said Evans scandalously. "That's why they call 'em December an' May marriages – they're spliced in December an' – "

"Don't let's be uncharitable," said The Miller. "Anyway, May is a lucky month to be born in."

To the wedding Mr Evans was invited. It occurred on a Sunday so as not to interfere with business, a brief honeymoon – "totally unnecessary", said Evans – was to be spent at Brighton, and the Happy Pair would be back in time to open the shop on Tuesday and to receive the felicitations of all old customers.

As a wedding feast it was, from Evans' point of view, a failure, for not only was Mrs Lube present in startling magenta, but Old Sam, his whiskers dry-cleaned, was amongst the guests. Mrs Lube was unaccountably friendly.

"I hope, Mr Evans, you're going to let bygones be bygones," said Mrs Lube.

"I hope so, I'm sure," said Evans stiffly.

"Remember what you owe to my dear gran'father that brought you up when you hadn't got a penny piece," said Mrs Lube sweetly.

Evans choked and gurgled.

"I beg your pardon?" he said hotly. "That old – your gran'father were a mere menial and dependant. I said 'go' and he goed – 'hither' and he hithered – "

Mrs Lube smiled.

"Your memory ain't as good as it was when you was young," she said cryptically.

Possibly it was the effect this outrageous statement had on Mr Evans that put into her head the idea which, subsequently, was to cause the learned man so much acute mental distress.

"I can only say," he exclaimed in wrath, "that I'm sorry for your education! You're like the celebrated orsstretch that puts its head in the sandy desert every time somebody tries to take a rise out of him. You remind me of my old friend Cardinal Rishloo, who made the celebrated French Revolution because he couldn't find how the dumplin' got into the apple!"

"You're very strange. Mr Evans," she said, her hazy ideas taking a very definite shape; "strange in your manner. It must be goin' to these meetin's in Stibbington Street. You're very strange."

"I'm treatin' you like a lady," said Evans, "an' I dessay that seems strange to you."

The Miller was not at the wedding, and to him Evans related the events of the afternoon.

"You shouldn't have gone," said The Miller. "You know that Smike and the Lubes are thicker than thieves."

The wedding coincided with a period of great activity at Masked Marvel Mansions. The Lincoln weights were out, and Mr Evans had heard of a horse at Newmarket that was being specially got ready for the race. Moreover, to meet current demands and to satisfy the craving of his clientele for their daily heart flutters, he had secured one of the grandest bits of information about a horse running at Kempton Park that ever came to mortal man.

The information came, as all good things in life come, by the veriest accident. He was racing at Sandown one day and heard two men talking about Suggo. Now Suggo, as everybody knows, is not the name of a new washing powder, but the registered title of a thoroughbred race-horse in one of the hottest stables at Epsom. There isn't a cold stable at Epsom, but this one was so hot that steam heating was a superfluity.

"Not today!" grunted one of the men. "Kempton – keep it to yourself."

Evans went along, and by the aid of his card and the number on the attendant's arm, identified Suggo, who had a careless look in his eye which suggested that this intelligent animal knew that he was not being called upon for any supreme effort at the moment. In the race Suggo was never wholly visible. He was eighth, ninth or tenth till the field came into the straight, and then, moving up to make a show, he finished a respectable fifth.

Consequently, a few days after the wedding, Mr Evans was in a position to send out to all clients new and old the following:

EDUCATED EVANS'
MYSTERY HORSE!!!
What a beauty!
What a beauty!
Educated Evans, the World's Champion Turf Adviser and
Racing Profit, begs to advise the following:
MONEY FOR NOTHING
This horse has been tried to beat the best horses at Epsom.
SUGGO on Friday.
Help yourself and roll up with your TMO's for 10s for
ONE THAT WILL WIN TEN MINUTES
on Saturday.
PS. This horse has been Revealed to me.

"What on earth made you put that?" asked The Miller.

"To make it mysteriouser," said Evans complacently. The public likes mysteries. An' I've gotta subconscience about this horse."

He went down to see the race. This time Suggo led the field for half the journey and then fell back, a beaten horse.

"Rapped himself," said the trainer glibly.

There was another Kempton Park meeting a few weeks later, and he had arranged that in this race Suggo should not rap himself or do anything to himself except get his head in front at the stick.

Evans accepted defeat with the philosophy of one to whom adversity was no stranger.

"Can't give 'em winners every day," he said when he saw The Miller that night; "but I got one for Monday that will Doddle It!"

To all clients (new and old) he despatched the following Hurry Up message:

EDUCATED EVANS

Owing to his last selection Wrapping Himself (hard lines, hard lines), Mr Evans, the highly celebrated Turf Expert, begs to send his friends one and all

MOUSE HOLE

for the Littlehampton Hurdle on Monday.

Go for your summer's keep.

PS. This horse is a Revellation!!

In the race Mouse Hole found its namesake and crawled into it, finishing last.

And then a sinister rumour flashed around Camden Town. How much Alf Lube had to do with it, to what extent it owed its circulation to the affected concern of Mrs Lube, how far certain disgruntled publicans, whose word is law, assisted in its promulgation, is a matter for investigation.

The Miller, in the course of his business, had to make a few enquiries concerning the whereabouts of two car rugs which had been absentmindedly abstracted from a garage; and in the course of these enquiries he came into contact with Toby Lyons, one of Evans' biggest and fastest supporters.

"Poor old Evans!" said Toby, shaking his head mournfully. "That only shows you what education'll do for you, Mr Challoner."

"What's the matter with Evans?"

Toby smiled sadly.

"Goin'," he said significantly. "It's too much readin' that clogs-up the head-piece, and naturally the brain won't work."

"Do you mean he's mad?" asked The Miller, aghast.

"Revelations," murmured Toby. "According to what I hear, he sits in a trance and hears ghosts tellin' him what's going to win."

Everywhere The Miller went he heard the same story. In some subtle and pernicious manner the authority of Educated Evans was being underpinned and undermined. He took the trouble to call on Evans, and that gentleman smiled at his warning.

"It's only the lower orders, the riff-raff and the what-not," he said. "I don't take no notice of what uneducated people say about me. If people are like the well known wife of the celebrated Julius Caesar, suspicious of everybody, well, let 'em be! See what they say about you, Mr Challoner."

"What do they say about me?" asked The Miller interested.

"They say you've got three rows of houses out of the money you've done hooks out of! I always say:'You're misjudgin' the man. I don't suppose he's got more than a row anyway.' "

"Thank you for your enthusiastic championship," said The Miller sarcastically. "Now take a tip from me, Evans – cut out The Children of the Sun and the subconscious mind, and keep to your old method of finding winners – putting all the names in a hat and sending out the first one you draw."

Evans was not offended.

He went to the Cow and Garter that night with the idea of establishing, beyond any doubt, his complete sanity. Yevers, the inimical landlord, was confined to his bed with an attack of gout, and the encyclopaedic barmaid had been replaced by one of greater beauty but less erudition. He could not but observe that, when he entered the bar, silence fell upon the habitués.

"Good evening, friends all," he said in his genial way, as he ordered his whisky and soda. "The weather's mild for this time of the year. We shall soon have spring here."

Everybody agreed.

"Spring," said Evans, "is caused by the world rotating on its own equinox, thereby not only causing day and night, but also summer, autumn, Christmas and other seasons, the snow on the North Pole meltin' an' bringin' about the floods, causin' great damage to life and property, see Sunday papers."

Toby, who was in the bar, answered him, and his voice was gentle, almost pleading.

"Don't you think, Mr Evans, it'd be a good idea if you gave up studyin' for a bit?" he asked. "It can't do your brain any good havin' all these thoughts in your mind."

Evans surveyed his whisky with a mysterious smile.

"You can't be educated without thought, Toby," he said. "Take Biography or the study of insects. Microbes cause all diseases such as headache, earache, ingrained toenails – which brings us to the question of electricity, which causes both lightnin' and lamps. Electricity can be caused by water – "

"By dynimos," said a husky voice in the background. It was Hoggy Main, who for three days shovelled coal in a boilerhouse. "Dynimos and wires."

"Dynamos are turned by water," said Evans.

"They're not," said Hoggy. "I oughter know – "

Somebody whispered a remonstrance to him and he was silent.

"Of course they're turned by water, Mr Evans," said Toby soothingly. "Everybody knows that."

"Everybody don't know that," said Evans, irritated. "Only a few people, which brings us to the question of the human figure, composed of heart, lungs an' important blood vessels, which together with bones and muscles makes man, woman an' child."

Everybody agreed with him at once. The barmaid stood at a respectful distance behind the counter, ready to fly, for she had heard of Evans' strange disorder.

"What about the subconscience mind?" asked the irrepressible Hoggy.

"Shut up," said Toby. "Don't annoy the man. You oughter be ashamed of yourself, Hoggy."

Evans waved aside the defence.

"The subconscience mind," he said, "as everybody knows except the ignorant an' the common, is due to the brain actin' without people thinkin'."

"And I convinced 'em," he told The Miller. "Nobody so much as argued with me. It's brains that does it."

But a change was coming over the fortunes of the World's Champion. First his local, and then, as rumour reached them, his more distant clientele, grew shy of his appeals. It is true that he gave three losers in succession and two of them started at odds on; but the foundation of their scepticism was planted deeper than in the vicissitudes of a prophet's fortunes. His temper was not improved by the fact that he could not walk abroad without being confronted with the poster advertising Old Sam's Midnight Special.

Hardnut!　　　　　　　Hardnut!　　　　　　　Hardnut!
5-1　　　What a beauty!
OLD SAM'S DOUBLE NAP!
Information *v.* The subconscience mind.
PS. Keep away from the Bogey Man!!

One old-established client wrote:

DEAR SIR: Hearing you have gone wrong in your head, please take my name off your list and oblige.

He sent a winner to his dwindling clientele, but it was not of a price calculated to re-establish confidence. In a fit of despondency, through which ran the red thread of panic, he sat down in his little room one night to study the programme of the coming Saturday, and as usual he limited his study to the race which had the fewest entries, because, as he argued rightly the smaller the field the smaller the chance of pickin' the wrong 'un.

This race, however, did not promise well. Bogey Boy was a certain runner, would start at 6-1 on and doddle it. Mrs Lipski, another prominent jumper, might possibly beat him, but wasn't by any means a certain runner. At the bottom of the little handicap was a horse called Iron Face. He didn't remember having seen the name before, and disconsolately he went back to Mrs Lipski, turned up his tattered book of form, scanned the training intelligence of the *Sporting Chronicle* and eventually made up his mind to risk Mrs Lipski. She would be at least 7-2 against.

In no happy frame of mind he drew a stencil towards him and wrote laboriously, and had reached the line: 'This one has been sent to me by my correspondent as the coop of the century,' when – Iron Face!

It came to him like the thunder of drums. Iron Face would win that race. A revelation…his subconscience mind!

Iron Face would win: he knew it as certainly as if he were watching the horse walking into the winners' enclosure.

All of a tremble, he threw aside the sheet and started another.

Educated Evans has had a tip straight from his Sub conscience Mind!

A Revelation!   A Revelation!

This horse will start at an outside price and Can't be Beat. Old and new clients all, you will never get another chance like this.

IRON FACE

IRON FACE

The morning after he sent out the revelation, The Miller came tramping up the stairs.

"Evans, you're going to let yourself in very bad unless you drop this revelation stuff," he said. "Iron Face is an old crock that has never jumped more than two fences in his life. He's up against the best 'chaser in the Midlands…"

Evans closed his eyes.

"Subconscience mind," he murmured. "Help yourself an' don't forget I've got a mouth."

Later he met Mr Izzy Izzyheim, the famous turf accountant.

"You're a regular money-getter to me, Evans," said Izzyheim with great joviality. "If Camdem Town only stands you for another three months, I'll be getting that new Rolls I promised the missus."

Evans shrugged his thin shoulders.

"There's things you don't understand, Mr Izzyheim," he began.

"How much money have you got?" asked Izzyheim, his eyes glowing at the prospect of easy wealth. "Because I'm willing to lay you all you have at s p and never send a penny to the course."

It needed but this to spur Evans to a frenzy. Diving his hand into his pocket, he brought out a disordered collection of pound notes and postal orders; put his hand into another pocket and produced a ball of paper which, unwrapped proved to consist of five £5 notes.

"Thirty-eight pun' ten," said Izzyheim gravely. "It's just about pay my expenses to Brighton for the weekend."

He had one or two sycophantic clients with him, and these were amused. At that moment The Miller came up and Izzyheim hastily pocketed the ready.

"I've just laid our friend s p to thirty-eight ten against his subconscience horse," he said, and The Miller shook his head in despair.

"Evans," he said, as he walked with him towards the Cobden statue, "do you know that half of the people in Camden Town never see you without tapping their nuts?"

"Let 'em!" said Evans defiantly.

He went hot and cold as people pointed to him, walking down the High Street that afternoon, and in a state of misery retired to his room and sat in the growing darkness, his head between his hands, deploring the insanity that had led to him parting with his capital. With bitterness in his heart he cursed The Children of the Sun; cursed the subconscience mind...

A hasty step on the stairs, and The Miller burst in.

"You lucky brute!" he said...

"Three runners. They laid seven to two on the favourite, seven to two against Mrs Lipski, and they both fell and your hair trunk won at thirty-three to one!"

Evans raised his haggard face.

"What a beauty! What a beauty!" he said hollowly. "Subconscience mind *v* pickin' 'em out with a pin!"

MR EVANS HAS A WELL SCREWED HEAD

As the field came round the pay gate turn, Mr Evans stood on one leg with a look of exquisite agony on his face, for Theoline lay last but one and 'Theoline: go heavy' had been his £5 Special, his £2 Guarantee and his £10 Occasional Beauty.

As the field breasted the hill Theoline was absolutely last.

"Not a yard!" said Evans bitterly.

As the horses came opposite the silver ring a change occurred – out of the blue shot a bolt and Theoline, threading his way through beaten horses, came with one effortless run to win in the end in a hack canter.

"That Lappy's the best jockey in the world," said Evans to his companion. "He's what they call in the French language a *'Multum in Palmo'*, which means that he's there if he's wanted. He reminds me of the celebrated Bill Archer."

Bill Iggson, his friend, was both polite and flattering.

"It's a licker to me, Evans," he said, "how you do it. You've got your head screwed on the right way."

Educated Evans purred: he was still purring when the red flag went up. After that he purred no more, for Theoline was disqualified for boring.

"What a jockey!" he said savagely as they made their way across to the station. "There ain't no jockeys nowadays – only butcher boys an' what-nots! Did you hear what I said to him when he came out to ride in the next race? That Lappy can't ride one side of a horse nor the other side either. He ought to be warned off."

At that moment Arthur Lappy, speeding towards London in his Rolls, was expressing the same opinion to the pretty young lady who sat by his side. He was a fair-haired young man with a rather nice voice, for his father had been a fairly rich trainer and Arthur Lappy had enjoyed an expensive education. And he had other hobbies besides racing. Margaret Drace – which was not her real name – was most anxious to talk about these, and listened with some impatience to her companion discussing quite another subject.

"Did you hear what that poor little devil said when I came out of the weighing room?" he chuckled. " 'Butcher boy!' And I am!"

"Who was he?" asked Margaret, who wasn't interested.

"A little tipster from Camden Town – a chap called Evans. Poor little blighter!"

Margaret sought to bring the conversation to the subject of emeralds. She had seen Evans: she had also seen Iggson and had been more interested in that prosperous figure than in his companion. But for the moment…emeralds.

"You shall see them one day," said Arthur Lappy, and forgot all about Evans in the discussion of his expensive hobby.

For he had a passion for the green stones. Some jockeys collect stamps, some bookmakers' bills, some children, but Arthur Lappy collected emeralds, as his father did before him.

He had a flat in Half Moon Street, a house in Newmarket and a shoot in Norfolk, for Arthur's income was a very large one. He had had several big strokes of luck and he never wasted what he won. He was chary of speaking about his collection to strangers, but Maggie was no stranger. He had known her three weeks, having met her at a party given by an actor friend; and because she never betted and never asked him for a tip, he knew that her heart was pure.

Evans, as the race special thundered towards London, elaborated his views on bad jockeys.

"It's ridin' flash that does it, Mr Iggson," he said. "These here jockeys go dissipatin' up in the West End when they ought to be in bed dreamin' how they can help the public. They're like the celebrated candle that burns at both ends. It's havin' no education that does it. They're ignorant. Ask Lappy where the North Pole is an' what would he answer. Ask him about Julia Caesar an' he'd be flummoxed. Take foreign languages – suppose you said to him 'Polly voo Francy', he wouldn't understand plain English."

No doubt Educated Evans had reason for his sourness. Theoline was his eighth consecutive loser.

Well might Old Sam's Midnight Special chortle with joy.

Don't be robbed by so-call Educated Amatchers, come to Old Sam, The Expert.

(Same address for sixty years).

"Don't worry," soothed Iggson. "You'll come out on top – you've got your head screwed on the right way."

It was natural that Iggson should comfort his unhappy friend. Even on ordinary occasions this stout and red-faced man never failed to favour Mr Evans with a friendly nod whenever education walked the pavement before Iggson's Fresh Vegetable and Seasonable Fruit Store although, as sometimes happens to a world's champion prophet and turf adviser, luck ran a little churlishly.

"You can't find winners all the time, Mr Evans," said Iggson pleasantly. "Don't worry – you go on trying to find 'em and I'll go on backing 'em! You're a man who's got his head screwed on the right way."

This was a favourite saying of Iggson's, and the highest praise he could bestow on any man – that he had his head screwed on the right way.

The very next day he stopped Evans as he was passing the shop.

"I've got a thing here that you'll understand, Mr Evans. I'm an uneducated man myself, but you with your headpiece will see what it is in a jiffy. It's art."

"Art," said Evans profoundly, "*Is* paintin', the same as the well-known Lanspear, him that did pictures of dogs by hand. Or it's statures, the same as the far-famed Ajax defyin' the lightnin' in Hyde Park, or it's musical pieces – see Moseark."

Iggson inclined his head.

"This is a stature," he said, and led the way into the back parlour.

On the mantelpiece stood a piece of bronze – the figure of a woman in long flowing robes.

"I bought it at the Caledonian Market, and according to certain things that's been said, it's art of the best quality."

"It's Venus," said Evans, eyeing the statuette with a frown. "The Venus de Marlow by the celebrated Michael Angleol."

The inscription on the bottom said "Hebe."

"That's Roman for Venus," explained Evans.

"I've been thinkin'," said Iggson, "that if anything happened to me I'd like you to keep that. Accordin' to what I've heard it brings luck – especially if you keep it in a box under the bed and don't tell anybody you've got it."

Evans smiled.

"I'm not superstitious meself," he said, "an' I don't believe in mascots. All you got to do if your luck's out is to carry a bit of coal in your pocket an' spit every time you see a peebald horse."

"I'd like you to have it," said Iggson solemnly, "when I'm gorn."

Evans murmured a polite hope that the day would be long deferred, and returned to answer certain abusive letters that had come to Goodwin Chambers in the past twenty-four hours.

A few nights later as Evans sat, a brooding, unhappy figure, examining the day's results, and wondering what perverse fate had induced him to change his mind and send to all clients old and new Black Velvet (down the course) when he had woken up with the fullest intention and determination to send French Star (won 100-7), a whistle from the mews below brought him out into the open.

"Only one for you," said the postman as the educated man flew down the steps. "It's a wonder to me you get any after the stumers you've been lumbering on to the working classes."

"No insolence, my man," said Evans haughtily. "It's the likes of us taxpayers that keeps the likes of you postmen."

He took the letter upstairs and opened it. It was written on aristocratically thick notepaper and had an embossed heading.

If Mr Evans will call on Mr Arthur Lappy at 7.30 tomorrow night, he may hear of something which may be of assistance to him.

Arthur Lappy! The far-famed jockey! Educated Evans was in a twitter of excitement, and scarcely remembered how the next day passed. At 7.30 to the second he rang the bell against the polished door of Mr Lappy's flat, and was admitted by a valet.

Lappy himself was sitting in his den, a handsomely furnished apartment, a little overloaded with the objects of art which he had acquired in his extensive travels; for Arthur in the off season was a great globe-trotter.

"You're the man who called me a butcher boy," said Lappy with a grin, "and I admit I rode like one."

For certain reasons he was in an exalted Haroun al Raschid mood, at peace with the world, his heart charged with a benevolence which, to do him justice, was not unusual, even if it was a little more intensified that night.

"I'm going to give you a winner, but I'm not going to make a habit of it. Range Rider will walk the three o'clock race on Friday."

"Do you ride it, sir?" asked Evans humbly.

"No, I don't."

Arthur paused.

"I often wonder how you fellows get a living," he continued.

Evans coughed.

"Personally speakin'," he said, "I don't understand myself how the lower orders, the hoi polloi, or what I might term the uneducated masses, manage to exist. Take art – "

He stopped suddenly. When he raised his eyes he saw on the mantelpiece the exact counterpart of Mr Iggson's statuette.

"Good lord!" he gasped.

Arthur Lappy was quick to notice his surprise.

"Have you seen one like that before?" He lifted the bronze figure down. "I bought that in Milan. There used to be a pair, but a servant I had pinched one."

Evans was momentarily embarrassed.

"I can't exactly say I've seen anything like it," he said discreetly, for Mr Iggson had a private reputation.

There was a ring at the bell, and Arthur rose quickly.

"You clear out," he said, and the reason for the hurry became apparent to Evans when a radiant young lady passed him in the hall, leaving behind the faint fragrance of those flowers which only the Paris perfumer knows.

An industrious man was Educated Evans that night. To all clients ancient and modern went forth the joyous tidings.

EDUCATED EVANS

GOODWIN CHAMBERS,

BAYHAM MEWS.

Still the World's Chief Profit!

Still the World's Chief Profit!

Still the World's Chief Profit!

Educated Evans has received from an inspired quarter a winner that can't lose!

A winner that can't lose!

A winner that can't lose!

Information v. Gaswork.

All clients who have acted honourable are advised to go for a big stake on

RANGE RIDER******

There was something so definite, so cocksure about this missive that even that astute judge of men and horses, Detective-Inspector Challoner, was impressed and came up to see Evans.

"Where did you get this?" he demanded.

Evans smiled.

"One of me correspondents at Lambourn – "

"It's not trained at Lambourn anyway," said The Miller, eyeing the prophet with disfavour. And then, abruptly: "Is it from one of your dupes? I saw you at Sandown with him."

"Mr Iggson," said Evans with dignity, "is one of my highest respected clients."

The Miller chewed on his straw thoughtfully.

"Did be introduce you to the lady?"

"There wasn't a lady," said Mr Evans.

"I'm inclined to agree with you," replied The Miller cryptically, but did not explain his mystery.

It is a curious fact that all Evans' tips were not backed by the people who purchased them. After a big win there was a surprising number of clients, especially those who had soberly and solemnly agreed to remit the odds to five shillings, who had forgotten that the horse was in the first race, or hadn't had the money to bet with, or hadn't received this letter. But this day, as he walked through the High Street, Camden Town, made splendid by a glorious and unusual sun, he was intercepted every few yards by earnest men who assured him they were going to back Range Rider, and that this was the last chance that he'd ever get any so-and-so money out of them if it didn't win.

Four o'clock brought the happy result, four-thirty the surprising price; for at the last moment money had come into the market for three horses, and Range Rider had started at 100-9.

Iggson was the first to congratulate his friend.

"I've always said…"

Mr Evans went cheerfully back to the flat, in thorough and complete agreement that his head *was* screwed on the right way, and that he lay under an everlasting debt of gratitude to that great and supreme artist of the pigskin, Mr Arthur Lappy.

That night… The young woman from Iggson's made a call on Evans; she chose the wan hour of 2 a.m. and was unconscious of the unseemliness of it all.

"Good Gawd!" exclaimed Mr Evans testily as he opened the door and peered forth into the rainy night. "What's all this about?"

A small, squeaky voice answered him.

"It's Evie – the girl from Iggson's, Mr Evans."

"Wait a tick," said Evans modestly, and put on his trousers in the dark.

He turned on the light, straightened the couch on which, a few minutes before, he had been dreaming that the City was won by a horse with an elephant's head, and, opening the door, invited Iggson's girl inside.

She was neither young nor comely, but she had always been Iggson's girl – serving in the shop in the busy hours of the day and cleaning the house in the afternoons.

"Mr Iggson's in trouble," she said in a hushed voice.

Words and tone told the dire story. Mr Evans made a clucking noise to express his astonishment – he was in truth staggered. It was common talk that Iggson did not confine himself to the sale of greens and that, beside the trade in apples, he did a little buying on the side. If you found a clock or a bit of jewellery and casually mentioned the fact to Mr Iggson in the privacy of his back parlour, you were certain of collecting a bit of money and no questions asked.

But Mr Evans was not a common man. He believed the best of horses and men – especially horses. He never gave credence to the stories which came to him, but at the same time he had ears to hear and heard.

None the less he was shocked.

"That's bad news," he said, and added politely: "The worst news since the Great Fire of London in eighteen forty-eight that burnt down the Thames Embankment."

"I see a fire engine as I was coming along," said Iggson's girl conversationally, but she returned to the cause for her visit. "They come an' took him out of his bed – The Miller an' two 'busies', an' Mr Iggson got a chance to speak to me just as they was searchin' his room an' he said, 'Take that stature orf the mantelpiece in the bedroom to Mr Evans an' tell him to keep it for me till further orders' ".

She groped in the big, soddened bag she carried and produced the 'stature'.

"Good lor'!" said the startled Evans.

Never in his wildest moments had he dreamt that the statue would come to him in such circumstances.

The tragedy of Iggson did not disturb Evans' rest. He accepted other people's troubles with the greatest philosophy. Iggson was a man of some property and could pay for a mouthpiece – he would not at any rate require Evans' services as legal adviser.

Evans put the statue under the bed and slept the sleep of the completely satisfied.

He had reason for his satisfaction, for the next morning's post brought the most generous acknowledgments of the service he had rendered to a world of suffering punters. New orders rolled in all the morning, and the heart of the educated man swelled with joy and gratitude to his benefactor.

And then he remembered the statue. Obviously it was the one that matched Arthur Lappy's – what a chance of paying back the man who had re-established him in the estimation of Camden Town.

To think, with Mr Evans, was to act. Wrapping the statuette in a piece of white paper, wrapping that again in brown paper and tying it carefully, he waited till night and, going down to Half Moon Street, he deposited his burden on the mat outside Mr Lappy's flat, rang the bell and made a hurried exit. Only the words 'From a Friend' were inscribed on the parcel; for Evans had no desire to complicate the case against the erring Iggson. No doubt, he reflected, Iggson had fenced the little bronze piece from the jockey's defaulting servant.

When he got back to the flat he found The Miller waiting for him.

"Did Iggson's girl come here the other night?" he demanded.

"No," lied Evans. "What's the trouble, Mr Challoner? When I heard he was inside you could have knocked me down with a feather."

"Emeralds is the trouble," said The Miller grimly. "We've got Iggson and we've got Lappy's old servant, but we haven't got the girl yet."

Educated Evans dithered but did not faint.

"Lappy's old servant?" he said hollowly. "What's he got to do with it?"

"They were Lappy's emeralds," said The Miller, unusually communicative for a police officer. "Apparently his servant had been pinching things for years and fencing them with Iggson – that's how he got to know there were emeralds in the flat. Twelve thousand pounds' worth."

Evans spent an unhappy night.

For three weeks he avoided High Street, Camden Town, and lived hourly in expectation of arrest as an accomplice.

One satisfaction he had – he had returned the statue.

And then the miracle happened. Iggson, brought up at the Old Bailey, was acquitted for lack of evidence, and came back almost triumphantly to Camden Town. The first intimation Evans had of the joyous news was the sight of the smiling Iggson standing in his doorway.

"Well, Mr Evans, I'm out. All the lies and perjuries of these busies didn't get me put away."

Evans was overjoyed, and said so.

"Yes, I thought you would be. You're a man with his head screwed on the right way and you know a thing or two, Mr Evans," said Iggson. "And if you don't mind, I'll take that stature."

The face of Mr Evans dropped.

"I give it away," he said.

"You what?" shrieked the greengrocer. "Give it away…who did you give it to?"

"I give it back to the bloke it was pinched from," said Evans, pale but determined. "As an educated man I couldn't do anything else – "

It was lucky for all concerned that The Miller had followed Mr Iggson into Bayham Mews.

"What was the trouble, Evans?" asked The Miller curiously.

Mr Evans was dabbing his nose with an ensanguined handkerchief.

"I'm not at liberty to discuss the matter," he said. "I tried to do this low feller a favour an' he hadn't got the education to see it."

The Miller was looking at him oddly.

"I'm not going to ask you any more questions, Evans, but I've got an idea that somebody left a statuette on Lappy's doormat, and if you're the man Lappy owes you a bit. For inside that statuette were twenty-five emeralds worth twelve thousand pounds."

Evans gaped at him.

"Inside?"

The Miller nodded.

"The inside is hollow, but you don't notice it if the head's screwed on the right way."

THE TWISTING OF ARTHUR
COLLEYBORN

One of the hardest things that any trainer can attempt is to speak encouragingly about any horse he trains. Everybody knows Colleyborn. He is one of those honest fellows with a shining face that everybody likes. He never bets and never encourages his owners to bet, and yet in some miraculous way he is a very rich man.

It is true that he has been known to encourage his brother-in-law to bet.

To the owner of Boopah he wrote:

Your horse is very well, but there are other horses in the race quite as well. I am afraid of Mawky's horse and I rather imagine Sir Peter Booley's horse may be fitter than we think. I should have a little bet each way if I were you.

On the other hand, he wrote to his brother-in-law, Willie Yegley:

DEAR BILL,
Get me a monkey on Boopah, and this time keep the wires back till a quarter of an hour before the set time. We ought to get tens to our money. Thank you for the cheque over Mouldy Boy. Love to Cis.

ARTHUR.

Now Colleyborn was terribly susceptible to the charms of what is sometimes described as the fair sex but is as often as not brunette. And amongst the many pretty ladies who had driven to London in Mr Colleyborn's Bentley to see a play, followed by dinner and dancing, was a certain Arabella, who was acting at the time as the assistant of a Cambridge doctor. That is to say, she assisted him by making out patients' bills and typing the evidence he gave whenever he was called upon to swear that the gentleman who ran his car into a lamp-post and wanted to fight a policeman was not drunk but was suffering from temporary dementia.

In course of time Colleyborn and his lady friend parted. He did not ask her for the return of his presents, because he had given her nothing more substantial than a Good Time.

Soon after this Miss Arabella went back to London to another job, and there the matter ended, for Arabella married – unhappily, as it proved. But the lady never ceased to ascribe the cause of her misfortune to the dirty, low and underhand treatment she had received at Mr Colleyborn's hands.

And then fate threw this vengeful lady into association with Educated Evans. And this at a moment when Arthur Colleyborn was preparing several winters' keep.

The racing world had been greatly mystified by the eccentric running of Grub Alley, the four-year-old son of Fleet Court out of Mudslinger. Grub Alley was (according to various journalistic estimates):

(a) A good horse,
(b) A rogue,
(c) Touched in his wind,
(d) Unreliable.

There were shrewd people who thought that he was being fiddled in preparation for a big handicap. Certain bookmakers who had no illusions and knew Mr Colleyborn better than his owner, issued urgent warnings to their clients not to lend their names. Grub Alley's owner, a bewildered man who never betted, was told by Mr Colleyborn that one of these days the horse would surprise everybody, and was content to let nature take its course. So were the turf prophets who, having tipped him a score of times, left Grub Alley severely alone. Which is just what Mr Colleyborn most earnestly desired.

Grub Alley was in the Newshire Handicap with 7st. 61b. when the curtain rang up on this present drama of Misplaced Confidence.

Educated Evans was a philosopher in all matters except love. When Eros aimed his tender dart at Evans' simple heart his judgment went out to 33-1 others.

"To anything in skirts," said The Miller, shaking his head sadly, "you are Blackberries on a Country Road."

"This young lady," said Evans soberly, "is Educated. I admit she rather resembles the Venus dee Milan – but beauty's only skin deep as the far-famed Cardinal Garnet Wolseley said. She knows more about anatomy an' bones than any lady I've ever met. She was clurk to a Harley Street specialist who lives in Newmarket an' what she don't know about blood capsules and other well-known microbes ain't worth talking about."

"Does she know anything about horses?"

Evans smiled pityingly.

"She lived in Newmarket an' nearly married three trainers," he replied crushingly.

"And she preferred to marry a gentleman who is doing twelve months for assaulting the police," said The Miller.

Evans was covered with confusion.

"I'm doin' my duty by her," he said.

"That's what I'm afraid of," said The Miller cryptically.

Was it entirely for her intellect or her helplessness that Evans attached himself to Arabelle Louker? She was pretty – whether like the Venus de Milo or not is a moot question. Nobody ever saw that lady wearing clothes.

They met by accident, which was the only possible manner Evans ever met anybody. She was waiting for a bus and he was waiting for a bus, and he said it was a fine day and she agreed. Then she said that the way bus conductors treated people was a positive disgrace and he agreed. She got off at the Cobden statue and so did he. He asked her to have a cup of tea and she said she would like one. And that is how it all happened.

Mrs Lube, who loathed Mr Evans and spoke of him disrespectfully on all occasions, referred to Arabella as 'Evans' latest pick up', and expressed her amazement that a girl so singularly attractive should so descend the scale of taste.

"From what I hear." she told her husband, "Evans is giving her work to do at the office. I wish I knew the girl: she might like to pick up a pound now and again."

"I could easily get to know her," said the husband hopefully.

The suggestion was not well received.

"Wimmin' have been your ruin," she said.

He looked at her thoughtfully and was inclined to admit the truth of this. But he didn't, for obvious reasons.

Mrs Arabella Louker was a nice girl, a pleasant companion and an engaging talker. She had been secretary to a Newmarket doctor when Joe Louker crossed her path and she was on the point of returning to the medical profession at the moment when Mr Evans dawned rosily upon a dreary world which was mainly populated by landladies who wanted their arrears of rent, and gentleman acquaintances who were anxious to contribute to her support.

"What I like about you, Mr Evans," she said once, "is that you don't insult me. I've got so tired of walking out with gentlemen and having to dodge round back streets so as not to meet their wives and children."

"I'm a man," said Evans impressively, "not like the well-known Crippen. I always say that if education does nothin' else it teaches you to respect ladies. As the highly celebrated Queen Elizabeth said to the renowned Duke of Wellington – "

"What about Newmarket?" asked Arabella, who was not especially interested in the great figures of history.

"I'll run you down tomorrow – I've ordered me car for six," replied Evans. "Not that I think you'll get anything out of Colleyborn. If I could only find out whether he's working a coop with Grub Alley, it'd mean a fortune in my pocket, Miss Arabella. Bee Face is a stone pinch with him out of the way – "

"He'll tell me the truth or I'll wring his neck," said Arabella sombrely. "Oh, if I only knew how to get my own back on the so-and-so."

On this evening Mr Alfred Lube made a great discovery and came post-haste to the Headquarters of Old Sam's Midnight Special.

"That girl he's walkin' out with is a married woman. An' she's a friend of Colleyborn. Her an' Evans are goin' down to Newmarket to see Colleyborn. She knows him an' I'll bet they're after Grub Alley."

"By train?" asked Mrs Lube.

"They've hired Winkworth's Ford."

Mrs Lube thought rapidly.

"You go down by train an' don't leave 'em out of your sight," she said.

And the next morning…

Brightly fell the morning sunlight athwart the one window of Adam's Apple Orchard, Bayham Mews. There was no sound in that salubrious *cul de sac* but the chirping of famished sparrows.

Evans turned in his bed and half awoke with that uneasy sensation of impending unpleasantness peculiar to gentlemen incarcerated in Pentonville Prison who have an urgent appointment with the executioner at 8 a.m.

This unease brought him to wakefulness, and he sat up, blinking. His table was piled high with the envelopes he had addressed on the night before; the duplicating machine that a child could work – but never had – rested on the floor; the sheet was ready, which properly placed in the duplicator, would enable him to announce to all the world that Bee Face had been tried two stone better than Cresta Run, and if a boy could only ride him, would come home alone for the Newshire Handicap.

"Good lord!" gasped Evans, remembering, and threw his shivering legs out of bed, covered them decently with his best trousers, which he drew from under the mattress, where they had been carefully laid the night before, and began his preparations for an early morning breakfast.

By the time the kettle was making unhappy moaning sounds, his spirits had revived; and when he had shaved and had a wash he was ostensibly like himself.

He heard the thump and splutter of the hired car at the end of the mews, swallowed his breakfast hastily, buttoned his shirt and put on his classiest tie, and though a walking-stick is not a particularly useful piece of equipment for a car journey, he took his nearly gold-headed cane from the corner, went out, locked the door and made his way to the Ford.

He picked up his lady friend ten minutes later – she was surprisingly punctual – and in two winks, as it were, the car was bumping through Epping Forest.

Evans seized the opportunity to explain the growing importance of exact information on the Newshire Handicap. There was reason enough for his anxiety. The Newshire Handicap had suddenly become an item of important public interest by reason of the fact that the wealthy Australian owner of one of the candidates had, under the influence of good cheer and other refreshment at a public dinner, announced that he would give the whole of his winnings – if he won – to the hospitals; and for the first time in its history the Newshire Handicap was the subject of ante-post betting. Which meant that there was as much dead meat in that race as in any of the Spring handicaps.

The Newshire Handicap had also been a subject of newspaper comment and analysis. More than this, Mr Evans had received enquiries from his clientele concerning this event.

"I know Colleyborn," said Arabella. "He's the sort of man who gives nothing away. If I could tell you, Mr Evans, what I've done for that man, you'd be surprised – typed his letters, et cetera, et cetera, and all I got was a fifteen shilling dinner and a nine shilling bottle of

Beaune! I've not so much as had a ring or a bracelet out of him. And if he's going to work one of his dirty tricks on the public, and I can get the news beforehand, it'll break his 'eart – heart, I mean."

"If it comes to presents – " began Evans, in a munificent mood, but she was one of those girls who listened best when she was talking herself.

"I wouldn't have married but for him," she rattled on. "I said to him: 'Arthur, if I leave you, you'll rue the day.' I said to him: 'Arthur, I'm going to get my own back on you if it takes me twenty years.' "

"What did he say?" asked the interested Evans.

"He just sneered," said Arabella, "and scoffed."

"A man like that ought to be pole-axed," said Evans passionately. "He's worse than the well-known Charles the Eighth who had ten wives and had their heads cut off and hung in a private room. He's worse than the far-famed Loey the Nineteenth, him that got into trouble over Lewdcreature Burgia, the female Crippen of Italy."

"He's a skunk," said Arabella expressively.

Newmarket bounced into view at last. Strings of horses wandering aimlessly about the Heath; tiny boys in tight leggings; bored trainers following their strings home, and discussing loudly the latest musical and other sporting matters.

"There he is," said Arabella suddenly. "Stop the car."

The car needed very little encouragement. It stopped. Arabella got out and walked towards a rather red-faced, youngish-looking man who was striding across the Heath in the direction of the town. Unhappily for him, he was not mounted.

"Oh, there you are!" said Arabella, and Evans thought he heard a groan.

He watched them strolling about the Heath, saw Colleyborn's arms raised in frantic protest, saw Miss Arabella shake her fist under his nose…Evans sat and purred. Never had he seen racing information being extracted in such a picturesque manner.

After a quarter of an hour she walked rapidly back to the car.

"You wait in the town and have a bite," she said. "Me and Colleyborn's going to talk things over."

"Does he know who I am?" asked Evans, in some alarm, realizing the terrible things that had happened to touts at Newmarket – he had once been shown a mound of earth which was locally called the Ditch, but which a trainer had told him was a secret burial place of murdered watchers.

"Yes, he knows who you are. You don't suppose I've got any secrets about my friends?" she said. "But Mr Colleyborn's a very nice man and you needn't be afraid."

Mr Evans found an eating-house.

When he had finished and got back to the car, the driver handed him a note.

"A boy left it with me to give to you."

DEAR MR EVANS (*ran the epistle*), I've had a very long talk with Mr Colleyborn; and he's realized what a terrible mistake he made by giving me up. He says that Grub Alley won't finish in the first three, but the other trainer's told him that Bee Face is a certainty. I'm sorry I can't come back with you, but Mr Colleyborn wants me to type a few letters for him, and for old time's sake and because of the Past I am willing to forget and forgive.

With this information in his inside pocket Educated Evans sped back to London, a happy man.

Alfred Lube, who had watched the arrival of the car, who had seen the coming of the note, who had been a witness of that poignant scene on the Heath, also sped back in greater comfort.

"It's all right, Emma," he reported breathlessly to his wife. "That girl's got the information for Evans, and we ain't goin' to be caught this time."

Wherefore did Old Sam's Midnight Special come out flamboyantly, recommending all clients old and new to go their limit, have their shirts on, and generally to support Grub Alley – and there were ten stars against Grub Alley.

A more dignified communication was that made by Educated Evans.

EDUCATED EVANS
The World's Champion Prophet and Turf Adviser
KEEP OFF GRUB ALLEY!
KEEP OFF GRUB ALLEY!
KEEP OFF GRUB ALLEY!

Mr Evans has been advised by his Newmarket correspondent that BEE FACE could win the Newshire Handicap with 11 stone.

DON'T BACK GRUB ALLEY!
DON'T BACK GRUB ALLEY!
DON'T BACK GRUB ALLEY!

He was not unnaturally annoyed when Grub Alley won at 7-1.

Annoyance and resentment went hand in hand on this occasion, and he carried his sorrows to The Miller. Inspector Arbuthnot Challoner listened unsympathetically.

"Your so-and-so tip cost me two pounds," he said savagely. "Arabella twisted you, you poor mutt! And she's received the price of her villainy! I saw Colleyborn's Bentley outside Woolworth's yesterday."

THE KIDNAPPING OF MR EVANS

There was a certain head lad who had a number of private clients. Which is not allowed by any of the rules of racing.

He was a purveyor of very excellent information, but he had few clients, and those did not advertise him, for a very obvious reason.

Then one day he came from the country to Camden Town to stay with a sister who had done very well and married into the laundry business, and to her he poured forth the sum of his trouble.

"I had three winners last week and got nothing out of it," he complained. "Now if I only had a bit of money and could advertise in another name – "

"What about the Lubeses?" asked his sister suddenly – for she knew Mrs Lube personally.

"Her grandfather's got a paper – I bet he'd do something for you."

The head lad cogitated this.

"What about this chap Evans?" he asked.

His sister turned up a nose that was by nature tip-tilted.

"Him!" she said scornfully. "He made us pay for a shirt he said we lost! I wouldn't have dealings with a common man like that."

So the introduction to the Lubeses followed. Mrs Lube came to tea and met the head lad, whose name – well, never mind his name. At first the conversation was general. Then the head lad casually mentioned his profession; then he remarked on the valuelessness of watching gallops if you can't make money out of them.

Mrs Lube listened and quivered. She stayed after tea and came again that night, and she and the wicked head lad talked head to head and the conference was in every way successful.

A week after this, Evans was watering the geranium that represented the garden of Abbot's Speed House. He was in a complacent frame of mind. He had sent out one horse that had won at 6-4 and one that had been short-headed at 100-8. Hard lines! Hard lines!

It was not his custom to purchase Old Sam's Midnight Special.

"Why should I throw away sixpence on *his* Five Pound Special?" he was wont to remark. "When I got information of me own *v.* pickin 'em out with a pin?"

It was The Miller who brought the most sensational issue of the Special.

"Good morning, Evans," he said pleasantly. "Seen this?"

Evans' lip curled.

"I never read muck," he said.

"That's why your messages to the deluded public are so full of spelling mistakes," said The Miller, and placed before the educated man the Extra Special Issue.

It was printed on green paper – which Evans wouldn't dream of using because it was notoriously unlucky. Evans picked it up and his eye was arrested by the hysterical headline.

Secret Information by the Grandest Informer who will give Winners Galore! No more Educated 6-4 chances! No more swank bluff and babble! No more Educated Humbug by a so-called prophet! News that nobody knows! Not winners you get from the newspapers!

Next Wensday!

Next Wensday!

Next Wensday!

The winner of the Colebeach Handicap!

Can't lose!

Can't lose!

> Can't lose!
> Send P O 10s to Winner Mansions. Little Hilington Street.
> Old Sam's Grand Winner!

"This," said Evans rapidly and indignantly, "is mere stuff and nonsense and uneducated twaddle! This is mere playgaring! This man Old Sam is a mere beer-eatin' patrician that ought to be in an asylum for goats. Education! Look at the spelling – look at the vulgarity and commonness of it! He's worse than Charlie Peace the far famed inventor of the Chamber of Horrors; he reminds me of the man they couldn't 'ang; he's – "

"What is the source of this interesting information?" interrupted The Miller. "Do you know anything about the winner of the Colebeach Handicap?"

"Do I know?" scoffed Evans. "Ain't I had Hambone from the boy who does him? Ain't I seen him with my own eyes beat Abbot's Speed in a trial?"

"No," said The Miller, "you haven't."

But Evans was not abashed.

"I got this horse from a gentleman who goes to the same barber as the owner; this Hambone could win this race an' laugh at the rest. He could win on a tight rein or a loose rein. He could be left at the post an' then trot it."

The Miller listened patiently.

"Hambone was scratched this afternoon – now tell me another lie."

But it took more than that to upset Mr Evans.

"Scratched – tut tut! An' yet, after what the owner told me, I ought to have expected it. 'Evans,' he says, 'I don't know whether to run this horse in the Colebeach or keep him for the Royal Hunt Cup,' he says. So I says to him 'Whatever you do, me lord, don't show the horse up' – an' he's took my advice."

"You don't know anything about the Colebeach Handicap," accused The Miller wrathfully. "Until you saw this paper, you had no idea that there was such a race."

Evans closed his eyes, hurt but dignified.

"I was goin' down to Newmarket specially to see it run," he said.

"It's run at Haydock Park," said The Miller unkindly.

Mr Evans might dismiss lightly the frenzied claim of Old Sam, but in his secret heart he was troubled and uneasy. Never before had Mrs Lube made so confident a statement. He sensed, behind the blatant claim, the very core of sincerity.

That night he pored over the entries. Elbowed, Mognato, Binny Bird, Sweep, Obah, Lucy Lala…

He paused at this. Lucy Lala was trained in a little stable that sometimes sent out two winners a year but sometimes didn't. The trainer trained a few horses, as he told everybody, for his own amusement and the amusement of his friends. Apparently they had an enlarged sense of humour, or else they got a lot of fun out of paying their training bills.

Evans shook his head. No, that couldn't be it. He went further.

"Happy Grin, Yangtse, Mogador, Bony Bertie…"

He conned and conned till his eyes ached. And as he studied and thought, he reached a conclusion. It must be Yangtse.

He began laboriously to inscribe a pronunciamento which commenced:

Information from my new special and secret watcher…

He finished his work and went abroad for refreshment. In the meantime:

Mrs Lube snatched the still wet sheet from her grandfather's hand. She too had been working a duplicator and had not observed the entrance of her ancestor.

"You're not supposed to read that, gran'father," she said sharply.

Old Sam, who could read just well enough to decipher

LUCY LALA★★★★

in big black type murmured his apologies.

"Is that the horse you sent us?" he demanded.

He addressed the head lad who, with Mr Alfred Lube, were the other occupants of the kitchen.

"Take this five shillings and go out, Gran'father," said Mrs Lube tartly. "And don't go stickin' your nose into business that don't concern you."

When he had gone the head lad emphasized the wonder of his tip.

"I saw this horse tried – it's the biggest pinch that ever looked through a bridle, and if it don't bring you – us – in a thousand pounds, I don't know what will."

He spent the evening telling them how fortunate they were in having met him. And whilst this was going on there was another and less pleasant meeting.

It is a fact that Old Sam, who occasionally described himself as the Seventh Wonder of the Sporting World, but who, in more modest moments, was content with the less provocative title The Wizard of Camden Town – this Old Sam was normally a gentle, almost humble soul.

But when Old Sam, through the strivings and pushings of Mrs Lube, developed into the proprietor of Old Sam's Midnight Special he was no longer normal. For normality to Old Sam was a condition of mild fuddlement, beer being the instrument of his semi-insensibility. Prosperity brought spirits; spirits aroused in him a fierce pugnacity which was not consonant with his advanced age. So that he never met Educated Evans in the street but that he hurled upon that man of singular erudition the most opprobrious and bitter gibes.

Evans bore his trials with a certain haughty dignity, until one day he was passing a quiet evening in that same White Hart. He was, in point of fact, instructing the mind of Miss Eveline, the new barmaid, whose mind was not quite as plastic as a large piece of wood.

"…take botomy. Tomatoes are fruit – very few people knew that. Take apples – or *pomme de terres*, named after the celebrated racehorse that I gave when he won at Ascot, or it may have been Goodwood, what a beauty! Take the day an' night, so called because the world, which is the shape of an orange, revolves round the sun once in

120

twenty-four hours. Take Shakespeare, him that wrote the pieces which we all admire – "

"Take Shakespeare!" grated a hateful voice. "You couldn't take Shakespeare if they paid yer!"

Evans turned his head slightly and looked significantly at the barmaid.

"He's had enough," he said meaningly.

"You couldn't take Shakespeare from the Cobden stature to the Euston Road," sneered Old Sam as he lurched to the bar.

"An' there ain't a 'orse called Shakespeare. Don't take none of his tips, miss, or you'll die in the work'us. A double scotch and a splash, miss."

Despite Mr Evans' warning, the young lady with the diamond brooch served the old man deftly.

"You're a swindlin' 'ound," said Old Sam with great gravity. "You're a common pin-pricking perishin' piecan."

He tossed down the fiery liquid. Mr Evans ostensibly ignored him.

"You're one of those people that can't find winners – Lucy Lala – what a beauty, what a beauty!"

"Eh?" said Evans, instantly attentive.

As instantly, as his ghastly error came to him, was Old Sam sober – and Old Sam sober was a gentle soul.

"What was I a-sayin' of?" he quavered passing his hand before his eyes. "Did I say anything I oughtn't to have said, Mr Evans?"

Evans' soul was filled with a great exaltation.

"You said Lucy Lala!" he said.

Which was a great mistake on Evans' part.

He saw Old Sam reel from the bar, and waited only till the door swung close before he followed.

Little he imagined, as he worked feverishly at a new composition advising all and sundry to

Bet blind on
LUCY LALA★★★!!!
Don't take notice of previous message sent in error.

that Old Sam, rather tearful, was facing his enraged relatives with the story of his blunder.

Midnight was striking when a knock came to the door of Mr Evans' flat. Evans opened it and saw a diminutive boy in leggings.

"Are you the celebrated Educated Evans, the World's Champion Turf Prophet?"

He seemed to be recalling a sentence well learnt.

"That's me, my boy," said Evans graciously.

"Lord Iggerman wants to see you urgent," said the youth.

Evans gasped. Lord Iggerman was one of the greatest of the owners.

"To see me?"

"Yes, sir: he says he don't want you to tip a horse of his."

That was quite understandable. Evans saw nothing remarkable in the request.

"Very good, my boy — where is his lordship?"

"At the Goods Yard," was the staggering reply.

"He's in his special train."

Evans was intrigued. He followed his guide through the streets — but it was some distance from the goods yards that the special train was waiting, and to reach it involved dodging officious railway foremen and traversing a bewildering maze of railway lines. And in truth, his lordship's special train had the appearance of being a string of goods wagons.

The lad climbed up and opened a door.

"In here sir," he said.

Evans swung himself up to the dark interior of the small compartment and as he did so, the door closed with a crash and he heard a key turn. He tried to open the windows, but they were fast.

In the darkness Alf Lube and the head lad watched happily.

At four o'clock the next afternoon Mr Evans woke from an exhausted sleep to hear the door unlocked.

"Hullo — what are you doin' here?" demanded a railway man suspiciously.

"Where's this?" demanded Evans.

"Salisbury – hop it!"

Evans crawled out and made his way to the nearest bar. If there was a law in the land, the Lubeses should sleep that night in Albany Street Police Station.

The plot was clear – they were stopping him sending out Lucy Lala…if only he hadn't sent out a horse at all for that race! Yangtse! What a horse to send!

All night long he'd been remembering that Yangtse was touched in the wind and couldn't gallop on hard going and didn't like left-hand courses and wasn't any good over a mile.

A newspaper boy shouted his wares, and Evans with a sinking and bitter heart went out to buy a paper. He opened it slowly and saw the headline:

A TRAGEDY FOR BACKERS

Yangtse wins Handicap at 20-1;

Lucy Lala, a hot favourite, finishes last.

Mr Evans drew a long breath.

"Information *v* gaswork," he murmured, and went inside again to refresh.

EDUCATED EVANS DECLARES TO WIN

Mr Evans had many detractors. He had some admirers who stuck to him through thick and thin: men who could see no wrong in him. For example, one Harry Wissell was such a man. He was a good looking and athletic young man who might have broken into the most exclusive circles, instead of which he broke into houses, occasionally with profit to himself – occasionally to disappear from town into what is euphemistically called 'the country'.

The secret of his adoration of the educated man was no secret to police headquarters. During one of the periods of his retirement Evans, who was a kind-hearted man, had come to the rescue of Wissell's aged and ailing mother. In other words, he had paid her fine when she was charged with:

(a) Being drunk and disorderly.
(b) Assaulting Police-Constable Jones in the execution of his duty.
(c) Doing wilful damage to the extent of £1-3-4 by tearing up the blanket with which she was supplied in the cell.

Moreover, Evans had written her defence, which she read from the dock and which began:

Your Worship, Situated as I am, the mother of a large family, I feel my position acute. For years I have suffered from giddiness, pains in the head, rheumatism and other excruciating pains too numerous to mention...

124

Anyway, she was fined, though the magistrate expressed his doubt as to whether he was wise in loosing her upon an unoffending world.

Mrs Wissell gained a certain sanctity soon after the release of her son by falling in the Regent's Canal and drowning herself; and Harry never forgot what he owed to his benefactor.

"Mr Evans," he said on one occasion, "*If* I could do you a turn I'd walk from here to Highgate Archway on me bare feet."

And he meant it. He did many a good turn to Evans, notably when Alf Lube, flushed with wine and victory – for Old Sam's Midnight Special had given three winners in succession – made disparaging remarks about the educated man. It was unfortunate for him that Harry was present.

"Educated Evans?" said Alf Lube, smiling pityingly. "Why, he ain't a man, he's no better than a bit of horse-radish! Education! I could talk his head off, before witnesses or private – "

"Here!" said Harry Wissell.

Alf looked round, but did not recognize danger.

"I'm talkin' about Educated Evans – " he began.

"You called him a bit of horse-radish," said Harry.

The landlord, recognizing the symptoms, leaned over the bar.

"Outside!" he hissed.

They went, Alf Lube unwillingly. He returned to the bosom of his family that night slightly altered.

"And that's what I'd do to anybody who said a word against you, Mr Evans," said Harry.

Evans grasped him by the hand.

"But if you see Mrs Lube you might tell her that I knew nothing about it."

"If I see Mrs Lube she'll be sorry," said Harry ominously.

Evans almost wished they would meet.

His friend had expressed only one regret: he could not help Mr Evans in his own particular business.

"I don't know no racin' people, Mr Evans," he said regretfully. "I wish I did."

"Don't worry, Harry," said Educated Evans, with a quiet smile. "I know 'em all. Take Lord Durby: him and me's like brothers. When I take off me hat to him he takes off his hat to me. Take the celebrated Lord Wool – what's his name – him that invented Johnny Walker. I've slept in his park often an' often."

"You do get about, don't you?" said his admirer, awe-stricken.

Evans smiled.

"It's education," he said simply. "It's known' hist'ry an' breedin' an' geography."

"If I ever get hold of a winner – " began Harry.

Mr Evans was amused.

A week later he was wishing somebody would get hold of a winner – for they had succeeded in eluding his own grasp.

So sure had Evans been that a certain thing would happen at Epsom that he had painted a new signboard for his door –

'Pendleton House'. In a fit of great depression he had painted this out, and was half-way through his task of transforming that lordly demesne into 'Embargo Chambers' when The Miller came in unobserved and stood silently regarding the artist's efforts.

"You're a bad sign-painter but a first-class liar," he said.

Mr Evans started and turned, blinking up at the newcomer.

"Bless me life and soul, Mr Challoner!" he said mildly. "You creep in and out like the celebrated Shylock Holmes, of Upper Baker Street, NW. You remind me of the far-famed Lady Macduff, who walked in her sleep – see Shakespeare."

"I'd hate to tell you what you remind me of," said The Miller gently, and added: "You gave Pendleton for the City and Suburban."

"The eleventh hour wire – " pleaded Evans.

"Was Pendleton," said the remorseless Miller, "and four fifty-ninth second tip was that same dilatory animal."

"I got to get me living," said Evans, and went on calmly with his fraudulent sign-work. "Them Lubeses tipped Kinnaird. If you find winners by gaswork you're bound to be right sooner or later. My information was that Pendleton couldn't lose."

"My information was that it did," said The Miller, "and I backed him on your advice! Men have been certified as mentally unsound for less."

Evans paused in his work and smiled.

"I got one for you at Newmarket next week that'll come home by himself. This horse has been tried – "

"Is it Frantic?" asked the ruthless Miller.

Evans admitted it was.

"How do you get hold of these stable secrets?" asked the detective-inspector with an exaggerated expression of surprise.

Evans was not embarrassed.

"I got it from a chap who knows the chauffeur who drives the car of Mr What's-his-name, the celebrated author of the play that the owner of Frantic acts in. It's all about crooks."

"It's a pity he doesn't know you, Evans," said The Miller, who was in his sourest mood. "He could write a play about you."

Evans smirked.

"I was thinkin' of goin' on the stage," he said surprisingly. "I happen to know a young lady who's an actress – at least, she's not exactly an actress but she does the young ladies of the chorus."

"Robs them or robes them?" asked The Miller, interested. "You mean she's a dresser?"

Evans nodded.

"It must be a wonderful life," he said, rising stiffly. "Her father keeps the Grey Dog down at Lambourn – well, he don't exactly keep it, but he's got a job there. I never had such information in me life," he said enthusiastically. "I got a horse running at Newmarket next week that could fall down, take a nap and then win. There's another horse that I got for Chester that's Home. Did you want to see me about anything, Mr Miller?"

The Miller wanted to see him very badly about something. Harry Wissler, notoriously a client of Evans, had vanished from London as though the ground had opened under him and swallowed him up. And coincident with this disappearance came a complaint from the Berkshire police that Highlow, an historic mansion, had been broken into and an article of value, to wit a nearly gold pencil, had been removed.

"Have you seen him lately?" asked The Miller.

Evans shook his head.

"No, Mr Challoner."

"Well, you'd better give him a wide berth," warned The Miller. "The Berkshire police are pretty certain it was he who broke into Frithington-Evans' place. He didn't pinch much, which was remarkable. Frithington-Evans was in the next room – you know him, don't you?"

Evans knew him very well.

Mr Frithington-Evans was one of those rich men who hated spending money. His meaness, his general unpleasantness, have been canvassed in earlier adventures.* He changed his jockeys monthly and his trainer every half-year, and lived the tortured life of one who was certain that he was being robbed all the time by somebody or other.

It fell to Mr Challoner to call on this gentleman, for he had a very wide acquaintance with the methods of the suspected man.

"Yes, sir – it looks like Wissler's work – he always lifts casement windows off their hinges."

Frithington-Evans stood by during the inspection, biting his nails.

"Why the devil don't you catch him?" he demanded irritably. "That's your job, my friend."

"So I'm told," said The Miller coolly.

"Don't be impertinent, please," snapped Frithington.

The Miller almost lost his inspector-ship and Mr Frithington-Evans as nearly gained a thick ear.

"He must have broken into the very next room to the library where I was sitting," said the aggrieved young man.

"Were you alone?"

"I was not alone: I had my trainer, Mr Bluson, here, and we were discussing – er – business."

* *More Educated Evans* (Tallis).

All the racing man in The Miller ached to ask him whether the business had to do with a certain maiden race at Newmarket in which Mr Frithington-Evans had two horses engaged – Blain and Woggle. That morning there had appeared a paragraph in the papers that Woggle was a doubtful runner, having picked up a nail at exercise. But Blain looked to have a rosy chance. Mr Frithington-Evans became communicative.

"To tell you the truth, Inspector, we were discussing a horse of mine – if you were a betting man I would advise you to back it – it's called Blain and it'll win on Friday."

The Miller murmured his gratitude.

Soon afterwards he went back to London to look for the missing Wissler.

Evans was dozing when the gentle knock came to his door.

"Who is it?" he asked.

"Harry – Wissler, Mr Evans," came the whispered reply.

Evans got out of bed and opened the door.

"Seen The Miller?" he demanded.

"I ain't," said Bill, "but I don't mind seein' him. I got a alibi the size of a house. I bin stayin' with a friend at Brighton as I can prove on me oath…"

His voice sank to a whisper… Mr Evans listened eagerly, punctuating the story of Harry Wissler with innumerable 'Bless my souls' and 'Good gracious me's.'

Frithington-Evans was not a very popular man with the rulers of the turf. There was one noble lord who, besides being a steward of the Jockey Club, had the dubious advantage of being related by marriage.

His lordship was a man with a grim sense of humour, and he had one hobby – he collected the literature of advertising and other tipsters.

On the morning the Highstreet Maiden Stakes was decided he met Frithington-Evans strolling in the paddock.

"Good morning, Snoopy." By this pet name was Mr Frithington-Evans called in the secret circles of his family. "Are you running Blain in the Maiden Stakes?"

"Yes," said Snoopy. "I was hoping to run both, but Woggle picked up a nail at exercise – "

"I read the paragraph. Why run him if he's unfit?"

Frithington-Evans shrugged his shoulders.

"He's only short of a few gallops and it'll do him no harm to see a race-course," he said. "Blain is a two-stone better horse, and of course I'm declaring to win with him. That is, if Woggle runs. I'm not so sure. My trainer said he's come to a decision this morning and send him on. He hasn't arrived yet."

"Humph!" said his relative. "Lexleigh was asking me whether he should back him."

"You can tell Lord Lexleigh with my compliments," said Snoopy, with his sweetest smile, "that he can back Blain without the slightest fear. I've been carefully through the list of runners, and I'm perfectly sure there's nothing in the race that can beat him."

"Humph!" said the steward again, and went on his way.

Frithington-Evans had not many friends, but there was still a large number of people who did not know enough to keep away from him, and from the paddock to the private stands he was stopped every few yards; and to all and sundry, friends, semi-friends, nearly enemies and the loathsome ones, he told all he knew – as he said – frankly and without reservation.

When the numbers went up into the frame, a board was also hoisted.

Mr Frithington-Evans declares to win with Blain.

Blain carried his first colours, was ridden by his stable jockey; and Woggle, who did appear after all, had up a stable lad and the second colours. Blain opened at 7-4, and was a tight 11-10 chance when the tapes went up.

Nobody noticed Woggle, for he was running on the stand side, until the field came into the dip, and then he was seen; but for all his second colours and his stable-lad rider, he was four lengths clear of his field. It was more nearly six lengths when they passed the post.

"Extraordinary!" said Frithington-Evans to the nearest scowling acquaintance. "I've never been so shocked in my life. I had my usual pony on Blain. We tried them twenty-eight pounds – "

"I don't believe in fairies," snarled his acquaintance.

To the paddock, after the 'All Right' had been called, came Snoopy's lordly relative and, taking him by the arm, he led him into a quiet corner.

"Great surprise for you, eh? Terrible shock and all that sort of thing?"

"I assure you, sir – " began Snoopy.

"Read this."

The steward took from his pocket a document which was soon to be added to his historic collection.

Frithington-Evans frowned and read.

EDUCATED EVANS.
EDUCATED EVANS.
EDUCATED EVANS.
The World's Winner Finder and Outsider Discoverer
A COOP.
A COOP.
A COOP.

Today everybody will be on Blain! It will be Old Sam's Midnight Special!

WHAT IGNORANCE!
WHAT IGNORANCE!
WHAT IGNORANCE!

The real pea in the basket is WOGGLE, who never picked up any nail at exercise, and will arrive in a horse-box after racing starts. His well-known and highly famous owner, Mr

Frithington-Evans (no relation to undersigned) will declare to win with Blain, and Woggle will pop up. Help yourself, and don't forget the family motto of Educated Evans is 'Information *v* Gaswork.'

Frithington-Evans turned white and then red.

"That damned burglar must have told him!" he gasped, and in the agitation of the moment did not realize his self-betrayal.

"Yes, I backed it," said The Miller slowly, "but I'm very anxious to know who your informant was. It wasn't by any chance a larcenist who's succeeded in persuading some Brighton friends to perjure themselves, was it? He didn't glue his ear to the keyhole while Mr Frithington-Evans was discussing matters with his trainer, did he? Come across, Evans, I'd like to know all about it."

Mr Evans closed his eyes ecstatically.

"Information *v* gaswork," he murmured, and added: "What a beauty!"

FOR EVANS' SAKE

Detective-Inspector Challoner strolled along the Hampstead Road, his hands behind him, a new straw clenched between his teeth, and an introspective frown on his face.

Nevertheless, he could notice the approach of Joe Maycart, and observe with satisfaction that, at the sight of him, Joe did not recall a previous engagement and turn back, nor did he cross the road to avoid meeting with his representative of the law. Instead he quickened his step and appeared eager for conversation.

"Lor, lumme, Inspector," he said breathlessly, "you seen Evans?"

"Not for two days – why?" Maycart's eyes bulged.

"He's gotta fur-line' coat! Fur all round the collar – an' gloves! When he come into the Cow and Garter last night, everybody took off their 'ats!"

News, indeed, but:

"Is there any particular reason why he shouldn't wear a fur-lined coat?" asked The Miller blandly. "Has anybody lost one?"

"Oh, no!" Joe made haste to free himself of the imputation that he was nosing on any man. "It's straight – he must have bought it off a man up in the Caledonian Market. They say that Mrs Lube's linin' Old Sam's ulster with an 'earthrug. But Evans – what a lad!"

The Miller had no intention whatever of visiting the home of learning that morning, but curiosity to examine the cause of such local excitement brought him to Marked Marvel Mansions.

He discovered Mr Evans in his shirt sleeves, for the educated man was turning the handle of the Patent Duplicator that a Child could Manipulate, and it was hot work.

On a peg driven into the wall hung The Coat. The very sight of it was enough to induce a mild perspiration.

"Business is doin' well," said Evans, pausing to wipe his forehead. "I'm just sendin' out to three thousand, seven hundred and forty-two clients the glad tidings about my Lincoln horse – Cora: fear nothing!"

"Where did you get the coat?" asked The Miller, examining the garment curiously.

"Sable," said Evans calmly. "Used to belong to the Grand Duke what's-his-name: sable or muck-squash."

"Muck-squash, I should say," said The Miller; "raised in a rabbit hutch. What's the idea? It's getting warm."

Evans raised his shoulders and smiled.

"I've a position to keep up," he said simply. " 'As a bird is known by his note so is a man by his apparelations' – Shakespeare. All celebrated people are classy dressers. Look at Bo Bungole, the dandy of Bath an' Wells. Look at the far-famed Lord Dishralli, the well-known Prime Minister. Besides – "

"Besides what?" asked The Miller, when he paused.

Evans coughed.

"My young lady likes it," he said, with an attempt at offhandedness.

The Miller's mouth opened.

"What, another?"

Evans smiled.

"This young lady's different," he said. "She's what you might call an 'eyebrow'. Very superior – don"t know nothing about racing – mad on classicals – poetry, picture paintin', artistic stone masonry – "

"Sculpture," said The Miller helpfully.

"Everythin' like that. She don't even know I'm on the turf – can't bear racin' – everythin' like that's low. But poetry – ! She's fair pot – mad about it. She likes mine."

"Yours!" said The Miller, aghast.

Evans went to his hanging jacket and took out a folded paper. He was flushed and his eyes were bright.

"I just dashed it off last night," he said carelessly. "Never knew I had the gift till I tried. It's funny how a person can have poetry inside him and never know it."

The Miller unfolded the sheet slowly and read the title.

'To a Lady of Manchester Square.'

"After 'Errick, the celebrated poem maker," explained Evans. "She's very fond of 'Errick."

"Eric who?" The Miller was wilfully dense.

"I don't know his other name," confessed Mr Evans. "It's probably a Nong de Plume."

The Miller read:

> *The world turns round in twenty-four hours.*
> *Thus causing the night and the day,*
> *also the seasons, hence the flowers,*
> *Or so the people say.*

"That's not bad," said The Miller.

"It's education," said Evans gravely. "My young lady's like that – she wears glasses."

The Miller attacked the second stanza.

> *Thou are not like Lewdcreature Burgia,*
> *The female Crippen of France,*
> *Thou art like the Princess of Surgia,*
> *Who gave every gentleman a chance.*

"Who is the Princess and where is Surgia?"

Mr Evans rubbed his nose.

"I made that bit up," he admitted. "Poet's licence."

"Issued by the Jockey Club?"

"Post Office," said Evans. "I've never seen one but I've heard of 'em. I put in 'France' because 'Italy' wouldn't rhyme."

The Miller resumed.

> *I worship the pavement where your fairy feet*
> *Pedestrianates so bright and neat.*
> *You're like the wife of the well known Julius Caesar*
> *And if she'll have me I'll try to please her.*

"That's wonderful," said The Miller, as he folded the paper. "All you want is something like:

> *If your mind is at sixes and sevens,*
> *Go to Educated Evans,*
> *Merchants of street corner rumours,*
> *Send five bob and get his stumers."*

"Who wrote that?" asked Evans suspiciously.

"Kipling," replied The Miller.

Now Evans had only stated a vital fact in the mildest possible way when he said that Miss Hortense Curryfed was no lover of racing. She had been ruined by the turf. Her male parent had done in two grocers' shops by his rash and hazardous speculations in this department of human activity. Her first young man had put the money reserved for the purchase of a home upon St. Becan in the Derby, thereby paralysing all prospects of domestic happiness. Her second young man had been driven to financial embarrassment when Pons Asinorum failed to get his nose in front at the stick.

To add to her horror and detestation of the betting habits of mankind, she lived in the same house – and worked for a high-class Oxford Street bookmaker.

Evans had met her in favourable circumstances at a very high-class film in the Euston Road. He went to the Regent under the mistaken impression that The Immortal Hour was a new comedy, and after he had survived the risk of being thrown out for laughing, he found himself in conversation with a sharp but not unpleasant-featured female who confided to him that she had seen the film twenty-five times. Luckily, he learnt of her antipathy to racing before he began to talk about himself – which means that she started telling him pretty soon after they were acquainted.

Miss Hortense was a governess – she also had taken out a poetic licence – and looked after the manners and morals of two violent children whom she described as 'handfuls.' She had, she hinted, a bit of money put aside for a rainy day and her grandmamma had left her a small annuity. Obviously a lady. She liked men older than herself; bits of boys she couldn't stand. They got on her nerves. Obviously a sensible lady.

"I'm in business for meself," Evans told her, and when he referred to his clients she was not sure whether he was a lawyer or a hairdresser. She was too well brought up to enquire. She liked strong, silent men, she told him. Evans could be strong but he could not be silent.

At nights – three a week – they walked or took a cup of coffee together at the Oxford Street Corner House, or saw an improving film. Evans saw all the improving films in London. All about Women's Souls and Fate and Railway Accidents.

Mostly the films were about heroic women who sacrificed their principles for the sake of the men they loved. This was Miss Curryfed's favourite theme.

So the courtship progressed and reached, as we have seen, the stage where poetry commenced.

And then the blow fell.

One night, Evans, returning from Lingfield somewhat short of temper and money, and with the knowledge that he had sent out to all clients old and new, them that had acted honourable and them that hadn't acted honourable, 'Binge – fear nothing' (the same Binge having refused at the first fence like a sensible horse), ran into Miss Curryfed. His race glasses were slung over his shoulder as he strode across the broad meeting-ground of Victoria Station – there was no excuse.

Miss Curryfed confronted him.

"Mr Evans – you are a common racing-man!"

"I just popped down – " began Evans.

"You've been horse-racing and betting – never speak to me again!"

Evans was not in his tenderest mood.

"Very well," he said haughtily, lifted his hat and strode on.

Now that his true character was revealed, Miss Curryfed had no difficulty in establishing the identity of the deceiver. Even her employer had heard his name, and spoke slightingly of him.

It needed but this to revivify the dormant romanticism in Miss Curryfed's bosom. Was she right, she asked herself? Was she doing her duty, she demanded? The memory of parallel cases oppressed her. She thought of the film heroines. She thought of the pure young girls who had sacrificed their lives and futures, had given up All that they held Dear, and had married fat and bloated millionaires so that their sick sister should be attended by the great specialist whom they really loved. In her mind's eye she saw the young and beautiful girl who, though she was loved by the rich, handsome and chivalrous leading man, stood by her poor and crotchety husband – quite a minor character – and endured All until he was providentially run over by a bus, when she married the rich and chivalrous suitor, and faded out on a long and lingering kiss.

Her mind was made up. The path of Duty was clear. That night for the first time she listened to the idle chatter of racing-men who gathered about her employer's table. She heard and shivered as they talked with coarse familiarity of strange animals to which they gave no name, referring rather to "that thing of Leader's" or "that so-and-so thing of Bennett's," but from the confusion of narrative emerged one golden thread. She recognized its importance by the low tones in which the information passed across the table.

"Poor Pup – keep it to yourself," said the informant, and her employer nodded. "And whatever you do, Joe, don't be a loser on it. They'll back it away, and you'll get your wires half an hour after the off."

Poor Pup! She bit her lip to suppress her emotion and, going up to her room, she put on a dark coat and a shapeless hat and made her stealthy way from the house.

It was very dark; rain was falling in torrents, but she walked rapidly on. Could this be she? Miss Curryfed wondered bitterly, going forth in the night to this racing-man, to tell him of a horse that would win. But it was her duty.

She raised her chin proudly, drove back the tears, and reached Bayham Mews without any of the misadventures which usually overtake heroines when they are about to do something silly.

Presently she found Masked Marvel Mansions and, climbing the slippery wooden stairs, listened at the door. No sound came from within except an irregular groan that sounded like a vacuum cleaner that was working in fits and starts. Evans was sleeping. She knocked at the door gently and, when no answer came, knocked louder.

"Hullo!" said Evans, struggling up. "Who's there?"

"Mr Evans?" said a voice.

"Yes, that's me," said Evans.

"Poor Pup," she said hollowly.

"Who is?" asked the indignant Evans.

"Poor Pup," she said again, and he recognized the voice.

"D'you call yourself a lady," he demanded wrathfully, "comin' here in the middle of the night an' callin' me names? Where's your education? Where's your dickyorum?"

"Poor Pup," she said again — "I do this for your sake."

He heard the sound of her feet on the stairs, and when he opened the door she was gone.

Two days later Mr Evans opened his newspaper and read:

$$
\begin{array}{ll}
\text{Poor Pup} & 1 \\
\text{Jellybag} & 2 \\
\text{Oh You!} & 3 \\
\end{array}
$$

100-9. 5-2. 6-1.

He clasped his forehead in despair, and there flashed upon him an understanding of that midnight scene.

All that day he paced in vain the pavement of Manchester Square, but she made no appearance. He remembered now that she was working for a bookmaker, and a happy sense of content and complacency came to him as he construed her action.

Two or three days later he was just dozing off to sleep when a tap came at his door.

"Joojah!" hissed a voice.

"Here, wait a minute, Miss Curryfed."

"Joojah – farewell."

She was gone when he walked out on to the rain-splattered landing. But this time he made no mistake. To all clients, ancient and modern, went forth the joyous news: 'Joojah – Fear Nothing'; and Joojah accordingly obliged – at a modest price, it is true, but, as Evans said: "I can't help prices."

Night after night he waited on a chair behind the door for the coming of his mysterious informant. A week passed, but he neither saw nor heard her.

While it cannot be said that Mrs Lube was without her own especial dreams, the type indeed that is very popular in certain cinemas where they are not so very particular, she had all a righteous wife's indignation at a philandering husband. Prosperity had come to her from an unexpected legacy, and Alf Lube shared in that prosperity to the extent that he was able to go farther afield into bars where he was quite unknown, and where there was no necessity to wait patiently for a friend to enter and ask brightly, "What's yours, Alf?"

And in the course of his wandering, Mr Lube, who was of an inflammable nature, had met with one who embodied in her gracious person all the attractions of a siren, all the supple grace of a mermaid.

Every afternoon and every evening Alf Lube lounged into the bar of the Dog and Kettle, and fixed his languid eyes on the beautiful manipulator of beer handles and deft turner-up of bottles. And they had private conversations not unconnected, on Mr Lube's part, with the money that had come into his family. It is true that he gave the impression that he was the sole legatee, and he also hinted in his subtle way that he was unhappily married to a woman who did not understand him.

Miss Vera, the barmaid, who was well acquainted with this type of husband, listened sympathetically; and when, one day, Alf laid a golden bangle on the counter, she took it with downcast eyes, which not only established in his mind the illusion of modesty, but enabled her to see that it was only nine carat. And from there on the friendship grew apace.

"I'm in the sporting line of business," said Alf. "I suppose you've heard of me?"

"You're not Educated Evans!" said Hebe, with interest.

"Him!" said Lube contemptuously. "I could lose him! No, I own Old Sam's Midnight Special."

"Go on!" she said.

He went on.

How far on he would have gone will never be known. Mrs Lube had her suspicions aroused from the amazing fact that her husband had innovated a new domestic practice: he washed twice a day. That, and the purchase of clean collars and the discovery in his pocket of a bus ticket, brought her like a bloodhound on his trail.

Miss Curryfed met the squat and stoutish lady on her way to Bayham Mews, and Mrs Lube was not only very angry, but confided the cause of her wrath to the first acquaintance.

"Thank your lucky stars you're not married, young woman!" she said tremulously.

Miss Curryfed had never thanked her stars for anything so stupid.

"Me allowin' him money, with four mouths to feed, an' him carryin' on with a ginger-haired barmaid, an' I on'y heard about it tonight! I barmaided her!"

"You should forgive your husband," said Miss Curryfed gently. "Marriage calls for great sacrifice – "

"Five bob a day beer money – what's that?" snapped Mrs Lube, who was returning from one of those occasional pilgrimages which the erratic affections of her husband made necessary.

"If you love him," murmured Miss Curryfed…"To know all is to forgive all."

"I'm not so sure that I do know all," said Mrs Lube darkly.

"Now I," said Miss Curryfed, "am doing something I hate for the man of my choice."

And, encouraged by the confidence that had been given to her, she told the story of those midnight visits.

"I shall never speak to him again, of course," said Miss Curryfed sadly, "but I must help him in his struggle."

"Is it Evans?" asked Mrs Lube, all her wrath against her worst half disappearing.

"Yes, it is Evans – Hubert Evans," said the girl softly, and wiped her glasses.

Mrs Lube almost stopped breathing.

"Don't take the risk, miss," she said earnestly. "You've no idea of the people that live down that mews. I quite sympathize an' understand, bein' one woman to another. I'll tell you what I'll do, young lady. I'll tell him! I don't mind dogs, an' I'm older than you…You'll find me waitin' at the end of the mews every night at ten o'clock – either me or my husband. All you got to do is to tell him the horse…"

Week after week Evans listened in vain for the light footstep on the stairs. Week after week he bemoaned the surprising and startling success of Old Sam's Midnight Special, which was sending out three-star winners with disgusting frequency.

THE PARTICULAR BEAUTY

Educated Evans had many promising clients. They promised him odds to various sums, and a proportion partly fulfilled their obligations and a large proportion deeply regretted that his information had come too late to be of any use to them, and finished up their letters of excuse with the pious hope that he would have 'better luck next time.'

"They're not actin' honourable," said Evans bitterly. "Here am I, goin' around happy as a king an' thinkin' of all the stuff that's comin' and here are they playin' robbers and thieves. They're worse than Amlet, the celebrated Danish gentleman – they say 'My kingdom for your guarantee special', an' when it clicks an' I ask for my dues they say 'Out dam spot!,' Is that fair?"

"It certainly is the limit," said The Miller. "Have you ever thought of suing them?"

"What's the good?" asked Evans. "I know as much about the lore as the next man – but what's the good? Take Marky Wirral. You couldn't get him to pay if you took Scotland Yard with you."

"Why don't you cut him off?"

"I do," said Evans gloomily, "and round he comes an' pitches a tale about his old mother – I'm too soft-hearted."

"And headed," suggested The Miller.

There is honour among thieves – it is when you get down to the punting class that you touch the deeps of human depravity and artfulness.

"I'm weedin' 'em out," said Evans. "I wouldn't be surprised if I didn't chuck this low connection an' open up in a classy neighbourhood – Edgware Road or somewhere."

He tried employing a client who used to be in the fighting business, till his backers went broke. Tom got a bit out of every dollar he collected. The first night he came back with a shilling he'd got from Nosey Walker and a string of hard-luck tales that choked him as he related them. The second evening he came back with nothing more substantial than a skinful of beer, and he spent the night sitting on the bottom of the steps singing doleful songs about women. The next night he didn't come back at all.

Evans gave up all hope of collection. He had other matters of routine to bother him. And then Lew Emmings, the well-known fighting man, a fervent admirer and defender of Evans, came to him with a suggestion, offered in all deference and humility, but Evans shook his head.

"I'm very sorry, Lew. I'd like to oblige you, but I don't have no more women about this place. They're snakes in the grass, as hist'ry tells us. Take Mary Queen of Scotch – "

"Rebecca's Jewish," pleaded Lew.

"Well, take the well-known Queen of Sheba – her that done in the far-famed Solomon by gettin' him to go out and fight the Hi-tites while she was goin' round with another man."

"Rebecca's a respectable girl," urged Lew.

"So was Cleopatra, whose needle we all admire," said Evans rapidly. "So was Lewdcreature Burgia – up to a point. So was Bonny Mary, the well-known Duchess of Argyll. So was the celebrated an' highly respected Queen Elizabeth, commonly called the Verger Queen. No, Lew, I like an' respect you, but I can't give no jobs to no girl. Besides, I've got to think of your sister's reputation, workin' alone with me."

Lew argued in vain. But the deposed and dishonest secretary was not to be replaced.

And yet there was need of clerical assistance. He had recently renewed his association with the Goods Yard, and there were forty

£10 Specials to be struck off every morning between ten and twelve, after the runners came up.

Then again, he found his accounts were in bad order. He had written asking clients to act honourable who had acted honourable, and said so violently and offensively; and he had sent out his special messages to people who were on the back of his book – or would have been if he'd had a book.

"It's system an' order I want," he confided to The Miller. "I'm goin' to keep a file so they can't chisel me."

The Miller looked at him suspiciously, but the joke was an unconscious one.

"But wimmin!" Evans shook his head. "I've been both stung an' bit, an' I'm rapidly turning into a mysograph – I am indeed, Mr Challoner."

"That sounds like a writing machine to me," said the puzzled Miller. "You don't by any chance mean mysogynist?"

"Mysogynist or mysograph," said Evans carelessly. "One's Greek an' the other's Latin. Lew wants me to take his sister – "

"Why don't you?" said the Miller. "Little Rebecca is very pretty, very capable and very straight. If you take my advice, you'll give her five pounds a week and a commission on all the money she collects."

Evans thought the matter over and sent for Lew, and that faithful man came breathlessly.

"She's a good clurk an' a good collector, Mr Evans," he said.

"She oughter be able to get a job anywhere, oughtn't she?" asked Evans suspiciously.

Lew hesitated.

"Well, I'll tell you the truth about Rebecca, Mr Evans. She ought to get a job an' she could get a job, but she's very touchy about the way people look at her. She's so beautiful, Mr Evans," he said earnestly, "that she can't allow nobody to get fresh with her, or cast aspersions on her. I've had more fights over Rebecca than I can remember. If a feller looks at her like this" – he leered – "home she comes to me and says 'Lew, I've been insulted,' an' out I go an' bash the bloke. A feller tried to hold her hand once in the City an' she had hysterics for three hours an' twenty-seven minutes – by the clock. But you're a gentleman, Mr Evans, an' as long as you're stern with her she won't mind that."

With some misgivings Mr Evans awaited the arrival of the Particular Beauty.

She was all that the Miller had said and more, having one of these svelte figures that one associates with film stars. She had fair hair and deep blue eyes, regular features and a complexion like milk and roses. Evans knew that it was going to be very difficult to be stern with her.

"Well, Miss – " he began.

"Call me Rebecca," she said with a dazzling smile.

Evans glanced at her brother to bear him witness that he had this permission.

She was immensely capable, too. Under her nimble fingers Mr Order took a long farewell of Mrs Chaos.

"She's a good girl," said Lew, as they walked down the High Street together, "an' I'd kill me best friend if he got fresh with her. I'd take him by the throat an' bash his head against the wall."

Evans avoided her all day, and when he did come into the office a set scowl was on his countenance and he kept at a respectful distance, lest by some mischance he touched that twinkling hand.

The next morning, armed with a list containing the names and addresses of defaulters and the amounts owing, she set forth. At three in the afternoon came Lew, with a respectable pile of money, which he put on the table.

"Rebecca can't come back today," he said gloomily. "She went to Harry Watson to collect the thirty bob he owes you an' Harry looked at her funny. They've just took him to the hospital," he added.

On the next day Toby Lowe, a hired porter, met the request of Evans' new collector for immediate payment with a light-hearted suggestion that he'd pay twice over if she's come and have a cup of tea with him. Ambulance bells rang loudly along Great College Street.

On the third day she came home in triumph with a bundle of pound notes, in various stages of cleanliness, and laid them before the frowning Evans.

"Only one man insulted me," she said brightly, "but Lew can't find him. I think he must have gone abroad."

Evans counted the money with a glow of joy.

"You're one of the nicest girls I've ever – "

Then he remembered with a chill and looked up. A look of cold doubt was in her eyes.

"I'm talking alejorically or pari-doxically," said Evans hastily. "Being educated, Miss Rebecca, you understand, I have to use all sorts of metaphorics an' poetry."

He composed his features to a scowl.

"I respect you as a lady an' as a woman of business," he went on rapidly. "You're a sort of machine, like a motorcycle or a beer engine."

Her face cleared; the deadly suspicion passed from her eyes.

"I'm glad you told me that, Mr Evans," she said seriously. "I shouldn't like to think you were Light."

"Light? Me?" Evans' face was contorted with stupefied wonder. "Why, Miss Rebecca, I'm no more light than the Reverend Hinge – him that put the cracks in St. Paul's."

"I loathe people falling in love with me," said Rebecca.

"At the same time," said Evans, his natural gallantry overcoming his fear, "It's not to be wondered at…"

And then, as the look of distrust reappeared:

"It's not to be wondered at that you do, Miss Rebecca. Personally speakin', I hate people to fall in love with me. The wimmin that's tried to hold my hand! The girls that chase me around!"

She was interested, possibly sceptical. She had every right to be.

"I didn't know you were so fascinatin', Mr Evans."

"In a way I am," admitted Evans modestly. "I suppose it's the education. But love don't mean any more to me that it meant to the celebrated and highly renowned Lewdcreature Burgia, the female Crippen of Rome, that done in her father with arsenic an' got pinched just as she was drawin' the insurance money. What a lady! Take B— Mary…"

"What's 'B' mean?" She was alert for insults.

"Bolshevik," said Evans quickly. "There's a woman that never had no love for anybody. She had her head cut off an' never smiled again – see Hist'ry. Take Cleopatra, whose needle we all admire: she that was stung to death by apses – a kind of needle that the Egyptians sewed their mummies up with. She found Moses in the bulrushes, and everybody used to say he had her nose! Which only goes to prove that the voice of scandal is the voice of the people – or in other words, *pro bono publico* – French."

He made his escape, feeling very moist under the collar. For the next two days he avoided his clerk and collector, insisting that her brother should accompany him whenever urgent necessity took him to his office.

To make doubly sure, he engaged old Mrs Tomwit, whose son was doing seven, and who had eighteen months to go to qualify for her old age pension, to come and sit in the office during Rebecca's working hours.

"She's all right," he admitted reluctantly to The Miller, "but she gets insulted. I wanted to send out Darling Mine for the three o'clock at Plumpton today, but I simply daren't say the words. But I got something for you on Friday – St Cheese. He'll start at 10-1 an' he's money for nothin'. I'm sendin' this horse out to all clients – "

"Old and new," murmured The Miller.

"To all clients," said Evans, "as my £10 Special. The Lubeses are sendin' out Ratrun, as I happen to know owin' to havin' a friend in the printing business. Ratrun don't."

"Don't what?" asked The Miller.

"Run," said Evans.

The days that followed were too busy for Evans to absent himself from the office. Lew came with him, and with the aged lady the room was rather crowded. Lew took his turn with the duplicator, and Rebecca worked like three women, too absorbed in her labours even to detect the least disrespectful glance.

Now the Lubeses were also busy, for an unexpected piece of luck had come the way of the owners, proprietors and editors of Old Sam's

Midnight Special. Mrs Lube, to her fluttering joy, had become acquainted with a real jockey.

To tell the story of how this acquaintance was made is like examining the ancestry of the modern holder of an ancient peerage. Mrs Lube's cousin, Arthur Stickleburn the schoolmaster, coached in his spare time a staff-sergeant of the Royal Army Service Corps who was working for his first-class certificate. This sergeant had a brother who was engaged to the sister of the young lady whom George Grob was walking out with. Now do you see?

To scrape acquaintance with George Grob was a fairly easy matter. He was a little man with a bullet head and a roving eye, who chewed gum, wrote his name with difficulty and patronized a Sackville Street tailor. He was introduced to Mr Stickleburn who, having shared something of his cousin's prosperity, found an opportunity to pass on his capture to Mrs Lube; and there was a great luncheon at an Oxford Street restaurant, which cost no less than £8-15 – including wine, at which Mrs Lube met the great horseman – Old Sam and her husband were kept in the background – and the friendship was sealed when Grob informed his hostess that Ratrun was something to bet on.

"But the papers say it won't start," said Mrs Lube.

Mr Grob smiled a cryptic smile.

"If you believe everything you read in the papers," he said, in his most original manner, "you'll go off your rocker! He runs and he'll win, and if any of your friends like to put me on a pony, I'll let 'em – that's a nice bit of fluff over there."

The bit of fluff who was really a bit of fluff gave him smile for smile, and thereafter Mr Grob's interest in racing and tippery evaporated...

"Them Lubeses," said Evans, "has gone off their nut. They're sendin' out Ratrun, an' I happen to know from the boy who does him that he's bein' kept for Cheltenham. It's gaswork – absolutely gaswork."

"If Ratrun is in the field," said The Miller, "your St Cheese will be beaten two fences."

"Fear Nothing," murmured Evans, and went on licking stamps.

The rivalry between the Evanses and the Lubeses was so keen and so widely canvassed in Camden Town that the knowledge that they were sending, with equal confidence, two horses for the same race, added a certain piquancy to the event. Once more Camden Town divided itself into the rival camps and, when the selections were known, the balance of opinion favoured the sanity of Old Sam's advisers.

Because Ratrun was a perfect fencer; it would be ridden by a crack jockey; and though the possibility was that 5-4 would be an outside offer, yet 5-4 in the hand is worth 1000-1 down the course. And it was also known, through some mysterious agency, that St Cheese was not on the job. How these stories came into circulation has never been discovered, but it is generally believed that the big book-makers in London employ a corps of fairy-tale-tellers to disseminate profitable news.

"He's on the job an' he's tryin'," said Evans when the story came to him. "I not only had it from the boy who does him, but I've had it from the barber who shaves the owner's uncle. An' if that's not good enough, what is?"

"I think I'll come along and see this animal perform," said The Miller, and Educated Evans showed every sign of relief.

"She's comin' down too" – he jerked his head towards Bayham Mews – "She's never seen a race."

"You're not taking her, are you?" asked The Miller quickly.

"Not me!" said the fervent Evans. "Am I mad? Why, if I bought her an evenin' paper she'd scream for help. I never even take me hat off to her when I meet her in the street."

On a bright, wintry day Lingfield has its claims to loveliness, and Mr Evans walked from the train with a light step and a light heart, confident that the sun would go down upon a great achievement and the roll of honour which included Braxted, what a beauty, and Eton Boy, Marked Marble (the danger) would be still further enriched.

The Miller had come down on his motorbike. He came across the paddock to meet Mr Evans.

"Ratrun does," he said.

"What?" asked Evans, startled.

"Run," said The Miller laconically.

Evans frowned, opened his evening paper and scowled at the list of probables.

"It's not down here," he said.

"It's down here," said The Miller, pointing to the stables.

"You can't believe half these newspaper writers tell you," said Evans bitterly. "Half what they say's gaswork an' the other half ain't sense. They're like the well-known Volytare, the celebrated French officer, who wouldn't get out of bed till somebody told him how he got in it!"

In the depths of despair, he went in search of his party. The delighted Rebecca was standing by the ringside, watching the horses parade, and Lew was explaining to her the significance of the numbers on the boys' arms.

"Isn't it wonderful, Mr Evans?" she said, her eyes afire with excitement. "I've never been on a race-course in my life! And nobody looks at you − that's the wonderful thing. I could live here all my life. I heard somebody say just now 'Look at her beautiful legs,' and of course I got awfully upset, but they were talking about a horse − weren't they, Lew?"

"So he said," said Lew darkly. "If I thought he'd been talkin' about yours, Rebecca − "

"I'm sure he wasn't: he was a gentleman − he had an umbrella," she said.

Evans could take no part in their joy. His soul was harrowed with the knowledge that he had expended £5-4s, to say nothing of £1-4s in telegrams for extra special clients, in despatching to the world the glad tidings concerning St Cheese. Undoubtedly Ratrun was on the job. He went and stared at him as he walked proudly round the paddock before the race. Compared with Ratrun, St Cheese looked − well, just like St Cheese.

The jockeys were coming out. George Grob, the last to appear, strolled across the paddock, swinging his whip nonchalantly; and it so happened that Rebecca stood not only in his way but in his line of vision. He looked at her and winked! And, what's more, Lew saw him do it! In a second he had gripped the jockey's collar.

"Here, what d'you mean by insulting my sister?" he demanded hotly.

"He winked at me!" gasped Rebecca.

"Didn't I see him do it?" asked Lew wrathfully.

"Let go of me," said Grob, "or I'll give you a punch on the nose…"

The Miller was the first on the spot, and his strong arms separated the contestants; not, however, before Grob's eye was slightly swollen and his nose ensanguined.

"I'll murder you when I come back!" he hissed, as he dodged under the rail…

A jockey with a black eye, a sore nose and a malignant desire for murder in his heart is no fit pilot for a high-spirited thoroughbred. At the third fence from the back stretch George Grob drove his mount savagely at a jump, took off too soon…and the race was over. St Cheese plugging away through the mud, held the lead he established when he came into the straight, out-jumped his opponent at the last fence, and scrambled home by a neck.

"They've sent the ambulance out for the jock," said Evans complacently.

Lew glowered.

"It's have saved 'em a lot of trouble if he'd a-come back," he said. "They wouldn't have had so far to carry him!"

THE LAST COOP OF ALL

"He's a rum-looking devil," said Lord Fanerly.

"He can go a bit, my lord," said the trainer.

The two-year-old under review was a leggy chestnut who had a poor neck, drooping quarters and bad hocks amongst other defects.

"He's the rummiest-looking devil I've ever seen – how is he bred, again?"

"By Short Cut out of Brief Survey, my lord."

His lordship beamed round on his three pretty daughters.

"I'll give any of you a fiver who finds me a name for this atrocity!" he chuckled. "All right, Mr Atkins; we'll let him run for the stakes."

Which was his lordship's favourite joke, for though he owned a stable of good horses, he only had one bet a year, and that was on the Queen's horse in the Derby.

And this is where the story of Mr Evans' last and greatest coop begins. Perhaps it began in the latter part of last year, when he earned the hatred and loathing of Mr Goolby. Ernest Goolby was a well-off man who owned a chain of public-houses and a string of comparatively bad horses.

But by some accident a good one came his way, and having fiddled with it for three months, running it down the course and out of its distance, he decided to have a go, and to this end he opened up new accounts all over the country. By ill-chance, Mr Evans either heard or pricked with a pin the name of this gem and sent it, amongst others, to one Issyheim, a shrewd bookmaker. Ordinarily, the fact that Evans sent out a horse made no more difference to its price than the printing of its name in the programme, but by a second mischance one of the telegrams despatched by Goolby and backing his horse each way, arrived at Issyheim's office in time for him to put through an enquiry to further bookmakers. They too had had telegrams – the phone to the course was set to work, and Goolby's horse started at 13–8.

Very unjustly, he blamed Evans, and after he had recovered from his six fits he set down to work his vengeance. He had in his stables a two-year-old by Newsboy out of Railway Tunnel. It was by far the worst two-year-old he had ever owned, but when his trainer suggested he should get rid of it, he shook his head.

"I've got a use for him," he said.

Ernest Goolby, as it happened, lived on the aristocratic fringe of Camden Town, so that Evans was something more than a vague personality. For three months this cunning man stalked his prey…

It was the habit of Detective-Inspector Arbuthnot Challoner to make a tri-weekly call on the educated man. He made no excuses for his peculiar conduct, for The Miller was rather superior to public opinion.

"Goolby," he said, suspiciously, when Evans told him the good news. "Isn't he the fellow who said he'd murder you?"

Evans smiled.

"We all make our mistakes, Mr Challoner," he said. "Take the well-known Napoleon Bonyparte, him that was drowned at the Battle of Trafalgar. Didn't he put his telescope to the wrong eye? Take the far-famed Mary Queen of Scotch; didn't she walk over Sir Francis Drake's cloak that he put down in the mud, an' didn't he stick a knife in her when she was saying her prayers in the highly-celebrated Tower of London? Take Lewdcreature Burgia – "

"I'm tired of taking that woman," said The Miller. "But what does Goolby want?"

"To do me a good turn," replied Evans promptly. "He's got no children, being a bachelor; he's got millions of money. He took a fancy to me the minute we met."

"In the dark, I presume," said The Miller unpleasantly. "Take my tip, Evans – that man is going to do you dirt."

Evans smiled again.

That evening he went to dinner with Goolby, and the magnificence of Mr Goolby's dining-room took his breath away. Never had Evans seen so much gold on so much purple wallpaper.

"The point is, Evans," said Mr Goolby, over roast duck with green peas and sage stuffing, which later was to cause Evans a certain amount of discomfiture and interrupt the smooth flow of his conversation, "the point is, I took a liking to you the first time I saw you."

"It's funny," said Evans. "The first time I see you, Mr Goolby, I ses to myself: 'There's an educated man.' You remind me of the far-famed Volta, the well-known French cricket – excuse me! – 'im that got Looey IX and the far-famed Mary Auntynette executed in the well-known B. Tower. You remind me – excuse me! – of the far-famed Rishloo, who is well-known to all the local inhabitants for his piousness and education."

"I'm going to make your fortune, Evans," said Goolby, as he poured out some of Gilbey's celebrated invalid port, "and I can do it if you'll keep your mouth shut."

Evans smiled.

"I've got the shuttest mouth in Camden Town, as all will admit," he said. "I've got stable secrets in me desk – excuse me! – I never could eat onions – that even the Jockey Club don't know anything about."

"I wonder if I *can* trust you," asked Goolby, surveying him gloomily.

Evans smiled again.

"I'm like the far-famed Michael Velli, the well-known Italian poet. What goes in me ears never comes out of me mouth – excuse me!"

Goolby went on to explain that he had in his stable a colt by Newsboy out of Railway Tunnel, and that this two-year-old could catch pigeons. He had tried this horse well enough to win any reasonable Derby, but unfortunately two-year-olds were not allowed to run for the Derby.

"If you sent this out to your clients you are a mug. If I were in your place," said Ernest Goolby solemnly, "I should get together every penny I had in the world; I should sell my furniture, I should borrow money from my friends, I'd even use any money I had that didn't belong to me. Now, I'm telling you this as man to man, because I want to do you a good turn."

"Naturally," murmured Evans.

"He's running at Sandown in a maiden race – "

"Are you backing him yourself?" asked Evans. anxiously.

Goolby shook his head.

"No, I've given up betting; I've taken a vow – or an oath, as the case may be – never to bet again. If I was betting, Evans, should I give you this information?"

"I'd better write down the name," said Evans. producing a pencil and paper. "Railway Tunnel colt – "

"No, no!" corrected the other. "I'm calling him 'Press Cutting': in fact I'm writing today to Wetherby's to name him. Come up and see me tomorrow, and I'll give you the latest about him. You ought to make enough money to sink a ship, and if you don't, then all I can say to you, if you don't mind my being offensive, is that you are a mug."

Evans walked back to Frantic Castle on air. Who knew the secret his bosom held?

He would have passed Inspector Arbuthnot Challoner without noticing him, but The Miller called him back.

"You been drinking?" he asked suspiciously. "Or are you in possession of stolen property?"

"That's a game I never take on, Mr Challoner," said Evans, good-humouredly. "No, I'm just going back to the Castle to have a bit of tea and a sluice. I got some work to do." He smiled mysteriously, and then, as a thought struck him: "Suppose I was to ask you to lend me a tenner, Mr Challoner?"

"I should pinch you, right away," said Mr Challoner promptly. "But seriously, Evans, you don't want to borrow ten pounds?"

Evans nodded.

"I got something I want to back," he said, mysteriously. "Something that I can't tell nobody about. Something that I can't send even to me five pound clients."

The Miller became suddenly interested.

"You're putting your own money on it and you're not sending it out?" he asked incredulously. "You're mad."

Evans was turning away with a shrug when The Miller called him back.

"I'll give you a tenner; in fact I'll send you two tenners, and you can put one of them on for me. I can see my life's savings going, but this is June, when even inspectors of police are entitled to go a little light-headed."

He was as good as his word. That very evening, he brought four crisp five-pound notes.

Evans put them into his pocket with an air of nonchalance which did not exactly tally with the state of his mind. For he had been very busy all that evening, and had been amazingly successful. Eighty-seven pounds of his own ill-gotten gains had been supplemented by no less a sum than £20 of borrowed money. To this must be added a sum of £30 that he had wangled – there is no other word for it – from the landlord of the White Hart, with whom he had been restored to friendship: and the prospect of what would happen when Press Cutting lost boggled his imagination.

He would dearly have loved to refuse The Miller's loan and investment. For if there was one person in the world on whom he did not wish to commit a petty larceny, it was an inspector of the C.I.D.

The next day added to his commitments by one of those extraordinary strokes of fate which may be recorded but cannot be explained. Mr Highbrite, the well-known wholesale confectioner of Camden Town, came to Evans and asked him if he would purchase for the same Mr Highbrite a small van which had been placed in Evans' hands for sale. The negotiations had been going on for a month, and Evans was getting a fiver out of the transaction, for the owner of the van was a very old friend of his.

157

Only for one moment, as he saw £75 placed on the table, in real money, did he falter – and then, in a spirit of restlessness, he clutched the money with a trembling hand.

"I shan't want this car for a couple of days, Mr Evans," said Mr Highbrite. "I'm going down to Brighton for the weekend, and I know I can trust you."

"I'm like the celebrated Caesar's wife," said Evans hollowly: "All things to all men!"

That night he saw Goolby, and told him in detail the manner in which he had accumulated £245.10s. He did not exactly explain the incident of the van: that sounded too much like robbery with violence.

Mr Goolby listened and internally gloated. If there was one man in the world he desired to put it across, it was Educated Evans.

"Go down to Sandown yourself, my boy. Don't trust these S.P. bookmakers; it'll only get about. Go up and down the rails and put on a tenner here and a tenner there, and you won't affect the price."

After Evans had gone, Goolby got on the telephone to his Epsom trainer.

"Run that nag of mine on Saturday," he said.

"But he's shin sore," protested the voice at the other end, "and even if he wasn't, he hasn't got a ghost of a chance of winning the Maiden Plate."

"Run him," hissed Goolby.

Goolby had three cronies, men who were as wide as Broad Street, but had never been convicted, and so it happened that these three men had also suffered irreparable injury at the hands of Educated Evans, for they had been in Goolby's coup that had gone astray.

To them he confided the story of his fell deed.

That Friday was a very anxious day for Evans. He was torn between love and duty. He had acquired quite a number of good clients – men of substance who would act honourable in the event of a win. Should he leave them in the lurch, or put them in the cart, or leave them out? The thought was intolerable. His oath of secrecy was one lightly to be broken, for Mr Evans was a God-fearing man who regarded all oaths concerning race-horses as *ultra vires* from the start.

He struggled with himself before he went to a wealthy poulterer, and then to an opulent furniture-merchant, and thirdly to a plutocratic dealer in second-hand clothes, and told them the tale.

"You're on the odds to a five," said the second-hand gentleman, "and I'll put in the telegram at the last minute."

The others promised almost as extravagant a reward.

Encouraged by this dream of easy wealth, Evans went further afield. He came back that night exhausted with his journeyings, but with the consciousness that he was on the odds to £60 with twenty-three reliable clients who had acted honourable before and would no doubt act honourable again.

On Waterloo platform next day, he met The Miller, and to The Miller he confided his intelligence.

"Give me my tenner back," said The Miller. "I can get a better price myself."

He ran his eye down the programme.

"You mightn't see his name there," said Evans, anxiously. "He was only named a couple of days ago."

"He's here all right: where did you get him from?"

"From the owner," said Evans, and The Miller looked at him suspiciously.

"That sounds like a lie," he said, "and therefore it is a lie."

The race was the second on the card, and there was a horse in the race called Jujube, and apparently all the cognoscenti had been waiting for Jujube ever since the moment he was foaled. For no sooner did a reckless bookmaker – and you know how reckless bookmakers can be – open his mouth and shout "6-4 on the field" than he was almost trampled to death by the rush of gentlemen anxious to relieve him of his surplus weath.

Evans waited till the market had settled before he sidled up to one of the loudest of the bookmakers, and then:…"I'll lay a thousand to sixty Press Cutting."

Evans held up his hand like a small boy at school anxious to call his teacher's attention to his necessities.

"I'll take yer," he said, huskily.

The great bookmaker blinked at him, momentarily paralysed, but mechanically put out his hand to take the money – a gesture which no bookmaker ever forgets until he is dead.

From another adventurer Evans took 500-40. His last penny was invested when he turned a moist face to meet The Miller.

"What price did you get?" asked that energetic officer of the law.

"Sixteens's and twelves's," said Evans.

The Miller sneered.

"They saw you coming," he said. "I got 25-1 all right to my tenner. Now tell me the truth, Evans: do you really know Lord Fanerly?"

"Lord who?" asked the staggered Evans.

"Fanerly," said The Miller, impatiently. "You said you knew the owner of Press Cutting."

"He don't own him," said the agitated Evans. "He belongs to Goolby."

The Miller scowled from Evans to the card.

"Here's Goolby's horse," he said – "No. 4. Colt by Newsboy out of Railway Tunnel!... Here, hold up!" – Evans had collapsed against him.

"I wanted to back Goolby's horse," he wailed. "Oh, my Gawd, I've backed the wrong 'un!"

The Miller shook him with an ungentle hand.

"You poor soused mackerel," he hissed. "Do you mean to tell me you've done in my tenner?"

At that moment the gate went up, and a crowd of silken-jackets jumbled together. Half-way it was impossible to tell which of six horses was leading, but a furlong from home the puce-and-green jacket of Lord Fanerly forged to the front.

"We've won," gasped The Miller. "You lucky rat!"

In the unsaddling enclosure Lord Fanerly was talking to a friend.

"Yes, he's a rum-looking devil, and the queer thing is that when I named him, there was another feller applying for exactly the same name, but I got in five minutes ahead of him.

"Not badly named, is he?... By Short Cut out of Brief Survey... A rum-looking devil!"

Edgar Wallace

Big Foot

Footprints and a dead woman bring together Superintendent Minton
and the amateur sleuth Mr Cardew. Who is the man in the shrubbery?
Who is the singer of the haunting Moorish tune? Why is Hannah
Shaw so determined to go to Pawsy, 'a dog lonely place' she had
previously detested? Death lurks in the dark and someone must solve
the mystery before BIG FOOT strikes again, in a yet more fiendish
manner.

Bones In London

The new Managing Director of Schemes Ltd has an elegant London
office and a theatrically dressed assistant – however, Bones, as he is
better known, is bored. Luckily there is a slump in the shipping
market and it is not long before Joe and Fred Pole pay Bones a visit.
They are totally unprepared for Bones' unnerving style of doing
business, unprepared for his unique style of innocent and endearing
mischief.

Edgar Wallace

Bones of the River

'Taking the little paper from the pigeon's leg, Hamilton saw it was from Sanders and marked URGENT. *Send Bones instantly to Lujamalababa… Arrest and bring to headquarters the witch doctor.*'

It is a time when the world's most powerful nations are vying for colonial honour, a time of trading steamers and tribal chiefs. In the mysterious African territories administered by Commissioner Sanders, Bones persistently manages to create his own unique style of innocent and endearing mischief.

The Daffodil Mystery

When Mr Thomas Lyne, poet, poseur and owner of Lyne's Emporium insults a cashier, Odette Rider, she resigns. Having summoned detective Jack Tarling to investigate another employee, Mr Milburgh, Lyne now changes his plans. Tarling and his Chinese companion refuse to become involved. They pay a visit to Odette's flat and in the hall Tarling meets Sam, convicted felon and protégé of Lyne. Next morning Tarling discovers a body. The hands are crossed on the breast, adorned with a handful of daffodils.

EDGAR WALLACE

THE JOKER
(USA: THE COLOSSUS)

While the millionaire Stratford Harlow is in Princetown, not only does he meet with his lawyer Mr Ellenbury but he gets his first glimpse of the beautiful Aileen Rivers, niece of the actor and convicted felon Arthur Ingle. When Aileen is involved in a car accident on the Thames Embankment, the driver is James Carlton of Scotland Yard. Later that evening Carlton gets a call. It is Aileen. She needs help.

THE SQUARE EMERALD
(USA: THE GIRL FROM SCOTLAND YARD)

'Suicide on the left,' says Chief Inspector Coldwell pleasantly, as he and Leslie Maughan stride along the Thames Embankment during a brutally cold night. A gaunt figure is sprawled across the parapet. But Coldwell soon discovers that Peter Dawlish, fresh out of prison for forgery, is not considering suicide but murder. Coldwell suspects Druze as the intended victim. Maughan disagrees. If Druze dies, she says, 'It will be because he does not love children!'

OTHER TITLES BY EDGAR WALLACE AVAILABLE DIRECT
FROM HOUSE OF STRATUS

Quantity		£	$(US)	$(CAN)	€
	The Admirable Carfew	6.99	12.95	19.95	13.50
	The Angel of Terror	6.99	12.95	19.95	13.50
	The Avenger (USA: The Hairy Arm)	6.99	12.95	19.95	13.50
	Barbara On Her Own	6.99	12.95	19.95	13.50
	Big Foot	6.99	12.95	19.95	13.50
	The Black Abbot	6.99	12.95	19.95	13.50
	Bones	6.99	12.95	19.95	13.50
	Bones In London	6.99	12.95	19.95	13.50
	Bones of the River	6.99	12.95	19.95	13.50
	The Clue of the New Pin	6.99	12.95	19.95	13.50
	The Clue of the Silver Key	6.99	12.95	19.95	13.50
	The Clue of the Twisted Candle	6.99	12.95	19.95	13.50
	The Coat of Arms				
	(USA: The Arranways Mystery)	6.99	12.95	19.95	13.50
	The Council of Justice	6.99	12.95	19.95	13.50
	The Crimson Circle	6.99	12.95	19.95	13.50
	The Daffodil Mystery	6.99	12.95	19.95	13.50
	The Dark Eyes of London				
	(USA: The Croakers)	6.99	12.95	19.95	13.50
	The Daughters of the Night	6.99	12.95	19.95	13.50
	A Debt Discharged	6.99	12.95	19.95	13.50
	The Devil Man	6.99	12.95	19.95	13.50
	The Door With Seven Locks	6.99	12.95	19.95	13.50
	The Duke In the Suburbs	6.99	12.95	19.95	13.50
	The Face In the Night	6.99	12.95	19.95	13.50
	The Feathered Serpent	6.99	12.95	19.95	13.50
	The Flying Squad	6.99	12.95	19.95	13.50
	The Forger (USA: The Clever One)	6.99	12.95	19.95	13.50
	The Four Just Men	6.99	12.95	19.95	13.50
	Four Square Jane	6.99	12.95	19.95	13.50

ALL HOUSE OF STRATUS BOOKS ARE AVAILABLE FROM GOOD BOOKSHOPS
OR DIRECT FROM THE PUBLISHER:

Internet: www.houseofstratus.com including synopses and features.

Email: sales@houseofstratus.com
info@houseofstratus.com
(please quote author, title and credit card details.)

OTHER TITLES BY EDGAR WALLACE AVAILABLE DIRECT
FROM HOUSE OF STRATUS

Quantity		£	$(US)	$(CAN)	€
☐	THE FOURTH PLAGUE	6.99	12.95	19.95	13.50
☐	THE FRIGHTENED LADY	6.99	12.95	19.95	13.50
☐	THE HAND OF POWER	6.99	12.95	19.95	13.50
☐	THE IRON GRIP	6.99	12.95	19.95	13.50
☐	THE JOKER (USA: THE COLOSSUS)	6.99	12.95	19.95	13.50
☐	THE JUST MEN OF CORDOVA	6.99	12.95	19.95	13.50
☐	THE KEEPERS OF THE KING'S PEACE	6.99	12.95	19.95	13.50
☐	THE LAW OF THE FOUR JUST MEN	6.99	12.95	19.95	13.50
☐	THE LONE HOUSE MYSTERY	6.99	12.95	19.95	13.50
☐	THE MAN WHO BOUGHT LONDON	6.99	12.95	19.95	13.50
☐	THE MAN WHO KNEW	6.99	12.95	19.95	13.50
☐	THE MAN WHO WAS NOBODY	6.99	12.95	19.95	13.50
☐	THE MIND OF MR J G REEDER				
	(USA: THE MURDER BOOK OF J G REEDER)	6.99	12.95	19.95	13.50
☐	MORE EDUCATED EVANS	6.99	12.95	19.95	13.50
☐	MR J G REEDER RETURNS				
	(USA: MR REEDER RETURNS)	6.99	12.95	19.95	13.50
☐	MR JUSTICE MAXELL	6.99	12.95	19.95	13.50
☐	RED ACES	6.99	12.95	19.95	13.50
☐	ROOM 13	6.99	12.95	19.95	13.50
☐	SANDERS	6.99	12.95	19.95	13.50
☐	SANDERS OF THE RIVER	6.99	12.95	19.95	13.50
☐	THE SINISTER MAN	6.99	12.95	19.95	13.50
☐	THE SQUARE EMERALD				
	(USA: THE GIRL FROM SCOTLAND YARD)	6.99	12.95	19.95	13.50
☐	THE THREE JUST MEN	6.99	12.95	19.95	13.50
☐	THE THREE OAK MYSTERY	6.99	12.95	19.95	13.50
☐	THE TRAITOR'S GATE	6.99	12.95	19.95	13.50
☐	WHEN THE GANGS CAME TO LONDON	6.99	12.95	19.95	13.50

Tel:	Order Line
	0800 169 1780 (UK)
	800 724 1100 (USA)
	International
	+44 (0) 1845 527700 (UK)
	+01 845 463 1100 (USA)
Fax:	+44 (0) 1845 527711 (UK)
	+01 845 463 0018 (USA)
	(please quote author, title and credit card details.)
Send to:	House of Stratus Sales Department
	Thirsk Industrial Park
	York Road, Thirsk
	North Yorkshire, YO7 3BX
	UK

PAYMENT

Please tick currency you wish to use:

☐ £ (Sterling)   ☐ $ (US)   ☐ $ (CAN)   ☐ € (Euros)

Allow for shipping costs charged per order plus an amount per book as set out in the tables below:

CURRENCY/DESTINATION

	£(Sterling)	$(US)	$(CAN)	€ (Euros)
Cost per order				
UK	1.50	2.25	3.50	2.50
Europe	3.00	4.50	6.75	5.00
North America	3.00	3.50	5.25	5.00
Rest of World	3.00	4.50	6.75	5.00
Additional cost per book				
UK	0.50	0.75	1.15	0.85
Europe	1.00	1.50	2.25	1.70
North America	1.00	1.00	1.50	1.70
Rest of World	1.50	2.25	3.50	3.00

PLEASE SEND CHEQUE OR INTERNATIONAL MONEY ORDER
payable to: HOUSE OF STRATUS LTD or HOUSE OF STRATUS INC. or card payment as indicated

STERLING EXAMPLE

Cost of book(s):.....................Example: 3 x books at £6.99 each: £20.97
Cost of order: ....Example: £1.50 (Delivery to UK address)
Additional cost per book:..............Example: 3 x £0.50: £1.50
Order total including shipping:..........Example: £23.97

VISA, MASTERCARD, SWITCH, AMEX:

☐☐☐☐☐☐☐☐☐☐☐☐☐☐☐☐☐☐☐

Issue number (Switch only):

☐☐☐

Start Date: **Expiry Date:**

☐☐/ ☐☐   ☐☐/ ☐☐

Signature: _____

NAME: _____

ADDRESS: _____

COUNTRY: _____

ZIP/POSTCODE: _____

Please allow 28 days for delivery. Despatch normally within 48 hours.

Prices subject to change without notice.
Please tick box if you do not wish to receive any additional information. ☐

House of Stratus publishes many other titles in this genre; please check our website (**www.houseofstratus.com**) for more details.